I0636774

Jersey Pines Ink

Presents

TREES

An Anthology

Edited by Dina Leacock

This is a work of fiction. Names, characters, businesses, places, events, locales and incidents are either the products of the authors' imagination or used in a fictitious manner. Any resemblance to actual persons, living or dead, or actual events is purely coincidental.

The publisher is not responsible for websites or their content that are not owned by the publisher

Cover art— Dina Leacock
Interior design—River Cove Production

For information, address the publisher at: Jerseypinesink.com

ISBN: 978-1-948899-19-2

Dedication

This book is dedicated to the small South Jersey town, Woodbine, where I spent my childhood reading books in the woods.

Mystery, Horror and Fantasy
Short Stories and Novels from
Jersey Pines Ink
https://www.jerseypinesink.com/

Seasons on the Dark Side, a Horror Short Story Collection by Diane Arrelle

Just A Drop In The Cup, a Collection of 42 Speculative and Mystery Short Stories by Diane Arrelle

WhoDunit, an Anthology of 42 Entertaining Mystery and Suspense Short Stories Edited by Dina Leacock

Crypt Gnats, an Anthology of the Horror Stories You've Been Itching To Read, Edited by Dina Leacock

The Chanting, a Novel of Supernatural Mystery and Romance by Beverly T. Haaf

Honeycomb Fire, a Novel of Adventure, Danger and Romance by Beverly T. Haaf

https://www.jerseypinesink.com

TREES

Table of Contents

Title	Author	Page
Wood Girl	Gargi Mehra	1
Between the Trees	Georgia Cook	6
Blame It on the Trees	Vonnie Winslow Crist	9
A Stop in the Woods	Claire Davon	17
The Weeds Grow Strong, Their Wordroots Deep	L. P. Melling	24
Mehlman's Revenge	Christopher Ryan	28
The Soul of a Tree	Donna J. W. Munro	35
Always Alone	Diane Arrelle	39
Into the Deep Forest	DJ Tyrer	46
Voices in the Wind	Ann Stolinsky	51
Tangled in the Tree of Ghosts	Tim Newton Anderson	57
Twelfth Pilgrim	Michael McCormick	64
Thoughts	Ginger Strivelli	68
Mom's Tree	John Cady	72
The Magical Forest	Shari Held	80
The Swamp that Ran Scarlet	Willow Croft	87
Tête de Bois	Liam Hogan	93
The Birchies	James Ryan	97
Where They Fear to Tread	Ray Daley	101
The Waiting Tree	Eric Fritz	108
One with the Forest	Kevin Hopson	115
The Birthday Tree	Adam Meyer	121
Rooted in My Next Life	Daniel Klim	127
Jodie's Spot	Mark Towse	132
Ant Lion	Matthew Hughes	140

Table of Contents

Title	Author	Page
The Divergence in the Woods	Dawn Vogel	142
Living with Dying	Kevin Brown	145
The Lonely Grave	Leonora Lewis	149
Bloody Sunday	Victory Witherkeigh	156
Red Oak's Revenge	James Blakey	160
Ties of Love	Lawrence Schimel	168
The Seedling	John Higgins	171
Golden Oldies	Christine Collier	178
Black-eyed Susan	Delfina Hex	181
The Secrets Trees Keep	Matt McGee	183
Balming the Thorn	Vonnie Winslow Crist	192
The Lonelist Tears	Michael H. Hanson	200

Wood Girl

Gargi Mehra

My lips run green on sunny mornings: a thick dark, almost emerald green. It alarms people because the rest of me resembles cinnamon. That's because I'm a humanoid, but not the robot kind. I'm what happens when a human being mates with a tree.

No, don't go all 'ew'.

It wasn't so much a physical mating as a chemical one. Most of the 'action', if any, happened in a petri dish. A sperm, an egg, and an injection of plant-based proteins and enzymes synthesized in a way that scientists had perfected after years of experimentation, or 'trial and error' as laymen call it.

The human beings that stroll past don't notice me. I sit most times upon a branch of my mother. She's not really my mother, but I call her that because I imagine that's what she would have looked like. I checked out a little book of trees, and inferred that the one whose sap runs in my veins must've been a banyan.

Sometimes, I descend from the branches and perch myself near the base of the trunk. People spot me, then blink twice, or shake their head. A few of them double-back to catch another glance, but I swoop upwards to the apex, where my body and the leaves merge into one. I'd live there forever, but Aunt wants me to attend school.

At the place she calls 'a temple of learning', I can't escape the stares. Grey-green eyes, skin the texture of bark—everyone calls me a freak. Aunt says, "Don't fret about that pack." But how can I not when their barbs chop my spirit into little twigs?

She's not really my aunt. I call her that because the powers-that-be have saddled her with my care, something she reminds me of almost every day at the breakfast table. Raising a humanoid child had never figured anywhere in her life plans, as she keeps muttering when she reads the paper, tightening her sweater about her and ignoring me as if that will make me vanish.

I don't know anything about my father and human-mother, except they're the ones who donated their bodily fluids to the act of my creation. I'm not sure my aunt knows who they are either, or maybe she does, and privately curses them when she pours herself a whiskey every evening.

As a child, I never had anyone pull my cheeks. People just gasped when they set eyes on me, even if Aunt hardly ever left me loose in the park or wheeled me around in a pram.

Now that I'm older, my classmates have grown used to my appearance, but they haven't warmed to me. The boys always tease—something about checking me for sap oozing out. I know what they mean, but I stay silent.

A girl who passed me an extra pen once asked why I was created. I don't know the answer, and I tell her that. There's no point in my sharing the theory of the government creating armies of us tree-people to produce oxygen, an element the earth has been falling short of for a while.

Sometimes I think of leaving the human world and running away to join the families of trees that live in forests. But the human part of me resists. The fear of the unknown handcuffs me to my present state.

TREES

At the age when other girls recruit friends to check the backs of their skirts for stains, the bark hardens between my shoulder blades. I stretch my hand far back to touch it, and my palms brush a rough growth.

At home, Aunt peers at it through a magnifying glass, and tsks. "I've never seen anything like it before," she says, "but then, you would bring unique problems into my life."

She carts me off to Dr. Scientist. That's what I call the man who, for human children, would have been just a plain old paediatrician. He resembles the dentists from toothpaste ads—wrapped in a white lab coat, rimless glasses thrust far back to the bridge of his nose such that his eyelashes flutter against the lenses.

When Aunt tells him about the growth, he makes me lower my shirt from the back to reveal it. I hear his assurance "this is just going to hurt a little bit" seconds before he punctures it slightly, and draws "blood and some muscle tissue so I can biopsy it."

Then he turns me out, and I flip through magazines in the waiting room, bending my head low over the words. That doesn't stop the other parents and children from staring at me so hard. One lady steps towards me, but by then the door swings open and Aunt bursts through it. She grabs me by the elbow and hurries me home. I daydream later that the lady had asked for my autograph and then stored it somewhere special, like between the pages of her diary.

The next day I find a hole carved out of my white shirt, to accommodate the protrusion. Aunt says it might expand more.

She's right, and it takes only a few weeks for the first branches to sprout. They're not heavy, so I go about my day as normal, picking up books and pens that the girls purposely knock down from my desk, and dodging the boys who reach out to grab the branches.

In the months that follow, I never need to look over my shoulder to check if stains are darkening my skirt, but a few more small branches emerge. Every morning, I admire the design that seems to grow out of me. My head looks like a sun that, instead of shining rays, has arms outstretched to hug strangers.

I start to wobble as the branches grow. They press down between my shoulder blades. Without knowing it I begin to hunch, even though Aunt sets me straight each time she spots me like that.

The day I faint in class, Aunt rushes to the school and hauls me off to the hospital-lab run by Dr. Scientist. They talk in hushed tones near the door. The words *unstable* and *loose* drift to my ears.

Aunt comes back looking concerned for the first time, and presses my hand as she sits beside me. They build a special bed for me, one that accommodates my branches and twigs. It's only a little more comfortable than the one at home. When I sit up, I catch a glimpse of the view outside the window. A cluster of trees sits in the center of the frame. I can't make out if they're banyans, but even so, I often dream of running away to join them. They'll nurture me, and I will surrender my tree-soul to the embrace of their limbs.

Dr. Scientist says they will conduct an operation, but they will run tests on me before that. I nod and agree. I need it too, considering my lips and body have turned greener than usual. Aunt appears at my side again, and squeezes my hand. A thin film of tears covers her eyes. I regard Dr. Scientist closely, but his face shows no expression, as always. Sometimes I wonder if he too is a humanoid like me, albeit one built from steel and wires. If I stripped off his lab coat and discovered a metal box underneath, it wouldn't surprise me at all.

Dr. Scientist and his team run their tests: hooking me up to machines, snipping off parts of my branches, observing them, taking more 'biopsies', as they call them. My friends don't call, they never call, but then I don't know why I ever expected them to.

The tests go on for months. The team cuts branches, but more grow in their place. The burden becomes too heavy for me to bear, so I must lie only on my side.

Once again Aunt and Dr. Scientist whisper between themselves in a corner of my room, careful to stand away from the machines and wires wound between them. This time I hear *close* and *final* and *time*.

Dr. Scientist heads back to me. It's time for the operation.

Aunt stands far from me, gazing out the window. Maybe tears are filling her eyes. It surprises me for a moment, but I can spare no more sympathy or time for her.

When they come bearing the long needle that would puncture the skin of my bark, I close my eyes, stretch out my arms, and in one swoop knock them down. The needle comes in handy to stab the minions nearest me, and my branches flatten the rest of them. The element of surprise works in my favour. Before I know it, I've stormed out the door and lumbered far from the hospital, the gown stripping off my body as I head towards my family. My feet carry me away, past the cluster of trees I'd observed from my window.

There, in the midst of the swampy wood, I rest my head upon the bark of my mother, and become one with her.

Between the Trees

Georgia Cook

My grandmother gave birth to Mamma in the woods, exactly equidistant between her house and the village, screaming blood and mucus into the moss, gasping lungfuls of loamy air, scratched red raw on blackberry thorns. She reckoned some vital part of my mother remained there, soaked deep into the soil, even after she'd been kissed and cleaned and washed of brambles.

I could believe that about my mother. Growing up, it was always I, not Mamma, who addressed the village folk, ordered our bread and milk, and saw to repairs; whilst Mamma sat in her rocking chair, owl-like, staring with her wide brown eyes.

There was something of the woods about Mamma. Something wild and unkept, even in her most tender embrace. She rarely spoke, rarely touched me. But whenever I cried, whenever illness gripped me, she would sit at my bedside and sing, sing, so sweetly.

That's how I knew she loved me.

I heard a story, once, of fishermen's wives down on the coast: spirits of the sea given form and a wedding band to chain them to the land. Spirits of spray and foam and raging depths, listening endlessly for the siren call of the ocean, who will walk one day down to the beach, step barefoot into the surf, and vanish forever.

In the days before my mother vanished, her embrace became as stiff as branches, her kiss as rough as bark. She did not speak of foam and raging depths, but her eyes grew distant, turning always towards the treeline. Away from me. Away from us.

The last I saw of her, watching from my bedroom window at the silvery night, was the white shape of her nightdress as she slipped from our cottage and vanished between the trees. Not once did she turn to look. Not once did she say goodbye.

They said it was such a shame, what happened to my mother. Such a terrible mystery. But it wasn't a mystery at all; I know exactly where she went.

And now I walk between the trees in the morning sunlight, tracing my mother's path.

Nothing stirs within the forest, but the trees watch as I pass. Sometimes they watch from above, with eyes made of swirls and knots, gazing across the horizon. Sometimes they watch from below, peering up through the bracken with eyes like spotted mushrooms.

They do not speak, but they watch.

There is a tree exactly equidistant between my cottage and the village. It sits behind high clumps of blackberry bushes and trailing ivy, tall and beautiful, silvery-slender in the morning light. Birds twitter among its branches, squirrels scamper back and forth across its bark; but under its shade there is always peace. Always stillness.

I reach the tree, clamber up between the branches, plant my feet on footholds and sturdy knots, climb higher and higher; until the world becomes a whisper of leaves and sunlight; until I am safe in its embrace.

Then I sit, and I breathe, and I listen.

Sometimes I wonder if something of my mother remains in the tree, if she remembers who I am, or if—like those tide-wives down on the coast—she was never meant for mortal form. I wonder if something of the trees remain in me; if one day I too will walk between the loamy shadows in the dead of night, and vanish forever into the green.

A breeze rustles my blanket of leaves. A bird flutters from branch to branch, chirping. Somewhere off between the roots, a squirrel sniffs the air.

The tree sings to me. It sings in a voice of leaves and branches, squirrels and bark. It sings like my mother. It sings so sweetly.

And I know, I know she hasn't forgotten me.

Blame It on the Trees

Vonnie Winslow Crist

Placing a natural habitat zoo in an urban section of town seemed counter-intuitive to Berg. A suburban or even rural area where the land was cheaper made more economic sense. But he knew first-hand the Victorians' love of city zoos with exotic animals from across the globe displayed in small, beautifully-formed, wrought iron cages. This zoo, like many, had originally been parkland dotted with trees, fountains, statues, and cramped Victorian cages that housed wild beasts.

The world changed. Outdated zoological parks were torn down and rebuilt one exhibit at a time. Nowadays, acres of open space and enclosures that were as close as possible to nature were all the rage. But the nearest zoo was still in a city, so, to the city was where Berg had driven.

After traveling up the twisting Zoological Park Lane, Berg pulled into a parking spot, turned off the car's engine, unzipped his camera case, and double checked his supply of batteries. Satisfied he'd be able to snap away with abandon, he looped the camera case's strap around his neck and slid out of his car.

Families with kids in strollers and backpacks paraded past him. Most stared. A group of young girls dressed in matching tee shirts skipped two-by-two towards the entrance. Scouts? 4-H-ers? Students from a girls' academy which held classes over the summer? It didn't matter to Berg as long as they did not linger too long in front of the animals, yawp at him overmuch, or disrupt his picture-taking.

After he had purchased a ticket, pushed through the turnstile, and walked to the polar bear enclosure, Berg took his camera from its case. The two bears lounging on rocks, and the one bear bobbing in the pool were whiter, bigger, and more playful than Berg remembered polar bears being. Of course, it had been years since he'd ventured into a zoo—too many people, too many gapes, too much commotion for his taste.

For about six or seven minutes, he focused, snapped, refocused, snapped, zoomed in, and snapped more photographs including one of the sign that gave important details about Ursus maritimus. Sure he'd gotten good pictures of the arctic mammals from several angles, Berg moved on to a monkey display. Before studying the primates, he paused briefly to pick up a discarded taco wrapper and place it in a metal trashcan shaped like a hippo.

The monkeys were putting on quite a show. Some of the troop screeched and flayed their arms. Others jumped from rocks to fake ruins and back again. The most boisterous individuals swung on ropes that dangled over the wide moat of dark water that surrounded their towering island and chattered at the people.

A small crowd had gathered around the monkey show-offs. Though Berg would rather have avoided the double-takes of the gawkers, the antics of the primates were irresistible and extremely photogenic.

It was while he was photographing the monkeys that someone tapped him on the forearm and inquired, "Would you help me?"

Berg lowered the camera, looked down, and found himself gazing into the hazel eyes of a short woman. At least, she seemed short when his seven-foot six-inch frame towered over her.

"I'm watching my sister's baby, and the wheel on the stroller is stuck. It looks like there is a thin wire wrapped around the axle. I can't hold my nephew and free-up the wheel at the same time."

"Ah, I guess so."

Berg was not used to strangers speaking to him. His height and bearish build intimidated most people. But this delightfully round woman with the wind-blown curls holding a squirming baby didn't appear to be put off by his size.

"I mean, yes. Let me see what I can do," replied Berg. He squatted, then lifted the stroller up. "Hmm. It's not wire. It seems to be a root or vine of some sort," he explained as he untangled a thin strand of vegetation from the axle of one of the stroller's front wheels.

Aware of the woman watching him, Berg's hands felt clumsy as paws. It took him twice as long as it should have to remove the viny rootlet. Once the stroller was again operational, he stood, still holding the offending plant part in his left hand.

"There you go. Right as rain."

Right as rain! Berg grimaced. Why did he always have to ruin every friendly encounter by saying something stupid.

The woman laughed, not a you're-odd laugh but a what-a-funny-thing-to-say laugh. "I agree. The day will be much righter if it doesn't rain." She quickly slipped her nephew back into the stroller and latched all the restraints in place. Then, she straightened back up, adjusted her wire-rimmed glasses, and tucked her unruly curls behind her ears.

"Thanks for your help."

"You're welcome," he replied. He felt like thanking her for ignoring his size and treating him like a normal person. Of course, he said no such thing. Instead, he lowered his head and started to move away.

"Want to keep us company while we visit the animals and enjoy the trees?" the woman asked. She patted a nearby walnut tree for emphasis.

Berg saw the walnut lean ever so slightly toward the woman.

"I, ah... " Berg studied her face. She was smiling and looking him directly in the eyes.

"Shelly," she said. She extended her right hand. "It's really Michelle. I was named for my mother. She uses Michelle, so I use Shelly."

"Berg." He kept it short. There was no use in explaining Berg meant mountain, and that he came from generations of tall people.

Several nearby trees looked in their direction and listened.

"This little sweet potato is Zander." Shelly reached down and caressed the cheek of the child in the stroller.

"Nice to meet you, Zander." Berg squatted again. He looked at the baby.

The baby made a gurgling noise in response.

"I noticed you taking pictures. Are you a photographer?" Shelly asked as they started to walk towards the grizzly bear enclosure.

"No." He adjusted the camera strap. "It's a hobby, though I have sold a few shots. Actually, I'm an accountant. I do taxes mostly, though I do audits several times a year."

"So you're good with numbers?"

"Yes." Say something else before she loses interest, he thought. But Berg couldn't think of anything clever to say.

"Not me." Shelly shook her head. Her curls bounced. "But I am good with words, so I edit publications for several companies. If you have a question about grammar or word-usage... I'm your girl."

"I will keep that in mind," he replied and smiled. He quickly pressed his lips together. Berg knew his teeth were large, unevenly spaced, and rather yellow. It wasn't due to poor dental hygiene, but rather to genes. Tooth color, like hair color, was a gift from your ancestors.

"You should smile more." Shelly tilted her head back and peered up at him. "You look so serious when you are frowning."

Berg scratched his forehead. "I am not a big smiler. Got ugly teeth."

"They didn't look that bad to... " Before she could complete her sentence, Shelly stumbled on a jag of uneven sidewalk.

Berg reached out, caught her under her arm with one hand, and grabbed the handle of the stroller with the other so it wouldn't roll away. "Steady there," he said.

Shelly held onto his forearm, then glanced down at her feet. "Looks like a tree root has grown under the sidewalk and split the concrete." Still holding onto Berg, she sighed loudly, then added, "I would have fallen if you hadn't been here."

"Lucky we met." He tried to sound lighthearted, but Berg was fairly certain had he not been there to catch her, Shelly would have gone sprawling, and the stroller would have rolled down the path. Who knows how badly little Zander might have been hurt when the contraption eventually tipped over.

The tree branches around them rustled. Berg noticed the aggressive tree root which had pushed up the sidewalk sank back into the earth. The sidewalk behind them returned to its normal almost-level flatness.

A dozen or so teenage girls picked that moment to pass Berg, Shelly, and Zander.

"Wow! Look at the circus freaks," said one of them under her breath.

All of the girls laughed.

"At least they've got a normal baby," another girl said.

"Yeah. Let's hope she doesn't grow up to be a giant or fat lady."

Again, laughter.

Berg tuned out whatever else was said as the teens pushed and shoved each other down the zoo path. "Sorry about that," he said to Shelly, who looked as if someone had struck her across the face. "Being so tall, I attract the wrong sort of attention sometimes."

The sparkle vanished from Shelly's eyes as she nodded, then said softly, "I am a little over-weight, so I guess I deserve... "

"I think you are just the right size." Berg cleared his throat. "I don't like scrawny women. I think women with some meat on their bones are beautiful."

Shelly gave him a shy smile, then straightened her shoulders, grasped the stroller's handle, and began moving towards the grizzly bears again. Without looking at him, she said, "I think big men are quite handsome."

Berg could not suppress a smile as he lumbered beside her.

As they rounded a corner and the Ursus arctos horribilis enclosure came into view, Berg observed the group of mean-spirited girls goofing around at the bear enclosure wall. One of the teens, urged on by her peers, had climbed on top of the wall and was pretending to fall into the pen. A zoo security woman hollered from the other side of the food-stall plaza for the girl to get down. It was at that moment Berg witnessed a maple tree push the girl into the grizzly pen with a quick swat of a heavily-leafed limb.

He raised his eyebrows. Trees were not usually that temperamental. But there was no time to consider the tree's behavior. The girls were screaming and pointing at their friend who'd fallen more than twenty feet into a rock-lined ditch. The grizzlies were moving closer. Perhaps it was just curiosity, but Berg realized it was likely one or more of the ursines would attack the unconscious teen.

"Someone needs to help her," Shelly gasped.

"Yes," replied Berg as he handed her his camera.

He strode forward. The growing crowd parted. Berg first pulled himself up onto the wall. Next, he lowered himself down as far as possible into the bear pen before releasing his grip.

Even at his height, it was a knee-jarring drop to the rocky ditch. He landed on all fours, then scrambled to the side of the injured girl. A quick check of her told Berg she was breathing, but unconscious. The teen's left leg was bent under her in an unnatural position, so he assumed it was broken. But the girl's condition was the least of his problems.

The grizzlies had drawn close—close enough he could see the whitish grizzled tips on their dark brown hair. One of the bears was slightly larger than the other two. Berg had no idea whether this was a family group or just a compatible cluster—it didn't matter. What mattered was the safety of the girl and, to a lesser extent, Berg.

Now less than twenty feet away, the bear trio had their mouths open and seemed to be panting. He supposed it was not only the presence of the human in their enclosure, but the smell of the teen's blood that was exciting them. Berg stood by the girl, raised his arms up and did his best to appear more enormous and fearsome than usual as he whispered a warning to the grizzlies in the Old Language.

The bears' ears flicked. They halted their forward movement.

Who knew when last they or their grandparents or their grandparents' grandparents had heard words spoken in that almost extinct tongue? But just as his mother and father before him, Berg had learned the Old Language so he could, when need be, speak to animals, plants, and even the rocks beneath his feet. Thus, he was certain the three Ursus arctos horribilis before him understood what he had whispered.

The biggest grizzly rose up on its back legs to get a better look.

Berg scooped up part of a log from the grass in front of him and launched it at the trio accompanied by the loudest, harshest-sounding curse in the Old Language he could manage.

The bears backed up.

Again, Berg raised his arms. This time, for the benefit of the onlookers, he yelled, "No. No. Back. Get back." He added, in a voice soft as a cold wind, a final warning to the grizzlies in the Old Language.

The bears glanced at each other, finally recognizing just who had jumped into their pen. The trio acknowledged with several huffing noises the long-held agreement between ursines and one of the ancient races. Then, without another glance at the injured teen or Berg, they turned and returned to the rock outcrop where they had been previously sunning themselves.

It wasn't long before the zoo's animal handlers lured the grizzlies back inside their cave-like cages. Then, medics and security personnel swarmed into the enclosure. The injured girl was carted away on a stretcher, and the abrasions on Berg's palms and knees were examined and treated. By the time Berg was escorted out of the bear pen, news cameras and reporters had arrived.

The crowd greeted him with cheers, handshakes, slaps on the back, and clapping as he wove his way back to Shelly and Zander. He tried to answer the questions the reporters peppered him with, but with the crowd cheering and the police anxious to take a statement, Berg found it difficult to talk.

Finally, one of the news crew pointed a microphone at Shelly and asked her what she thought of Berg's actions.

"I knew he had a giant heart earlier today when he helped Zander and me," she said.

The trees behind her swayed.

Then, turning slightly in his direction, she added, "I just didn't know his courage was giant-sized, too."

Giant-sized, mused Bergrisi Jotnar as a particularly gnarled beech tree leaned down and gave the woman and child a little extra shade on this hot summer's day. Shelly didn't know how right she was. Or maybe, he thought as he gazed into her clear, hazel eyes, she had recognized exactly who he was, and did not mind.

As he smiled his crooked-toothed, yellow smile and took Shelly's small hand in his gigantic one, Berg witnessed all the nearby trees nod their approval.

A Stop in the Woods

Claire Davon

Carina flopped down on a tree stump and closed her eyes. She jerked her backpack off and dropped it to the ground.

Jared's feet kicked up leaves and loose soil as he corrected the step he'd been about to make in favor of halting.

He'd hoped to get all the way to the campgrounds before stopping, but she'd clearly hit her limit. Jared hesitated, then shrugged out of his pack, letting it fall to the dirt with a thump.

"Here," he said, pulling out a bottle of water, and handing it to her. Carina took it, and drank half the contents before laying back on the stump. Jared measured the time. They had an hour or so until dusk, and still needed to set up their equipment once they made it to their destination. Impatience would do him no good. If he approached her the wrong way, then she'd insist she'd be just fine where she was.

He didn't have an option. Despite the shortage of time and their need to get to camp, they were going to stop. Right here, right now.

"We've gone miles and miles and miles already," she complained. "Can't we just call rideshare or something? This isn't fun anymore."

This had been a mistake.

"We're close," he said, grateful for the opening. "Just a little further, and then we're at the campgrounds. If we go now, we'll be there before we know it. I've even got wine for when we are settled."

That didn't even prompt a tiny tug of a smile.

A rustle of movement in the leaves made Carina's eyes fly open. "What was that?" She squinted toward the sun that came in through the tops of trees.

He peered into the brush, though he couldn't see anything. "There's lots of wildlife here. It didn't sound big, like a mountain lion or a bear. It might be a chipmunk, or maybe a vole."

"Vole? What the heck is a vole anyway?"

He recognized that she was gearing up for a fight. It had been a mistake to suggest camping. He wasn't sure why she agreed.

"Small creature, looks like a mouse, but with bigger teeth."

The crackle came again. Carina let out a vole-like squeak, and sat up. Her gaze darted about, examining the forest.

"What the fuck is it, Jared?"

"No clue. Let's get to the campground. There won't be any voles or bears either if you tie your food up into the trees." He didn't say that a bear would still get into their stuff. She had no need to learn that information.

"Bear?" She seized on the word like a drowning person plunging their rescuer under. "We're being hunted by a bear?" She grabbed for her pack.

"Doubtful," he said. *Possibly*, he thought.

The rustling came again, from more than one direction. Jared's heart also began to pound. He had hiked a thousand times, and never been in danger. If they encountered an animal bigger than themselves, their one option might be to run.

"What is that, Jared?" She tried to get her legs onto the stump to wrap her arms around them, but it was slippery with moss. She pinwheeled, catching herself before she fell.

"We should go. Trust me, Carina. I've gone to this spot many times. It's not too far now."

His racing pulse got faster, and he started to sweat despite the cool of the old growth forest.

"Should we? Bears chase folks when they run, right?"

Her voice held hysteria, the kind of panic that led people to breaking bones. The trees were everywhere, their branches and leaves getting in the way. They pressed down on him like their canopy was going to reach down and attack them.

Those women who were trees, what were they called? Jared couldn't recall.

He took several deep, calming breaths, and attempted to think in a rational way. Trees didn't eat humans.

Bears did, though.

She got her feet under her, and gave him a dirty glare when she got up, shaking off his offer of a hand.

"We should run." Her voice shook.

"Lots of predators chase things when they flee. That's what they do." He needed to be the reasonable one here.

"You brought me to a place where a bear might eat me?" Her voice had that hysterical edge again. Jared wished he could roll back time, and forget he'd ever suggested this outing. He hoped it might bring them closer. They could roast s'mores over a campfire and marvel at the stars while cuddling. That idea was ashes in his mind as Carina folded her arms, her face drawing into mulish lines.

"I've done this a hundred times, and never gotten eaten. Maybe by mosquitos, but that's why I doused us with repellent before we left."

She huffed out a breath, and shouldered her pack. Carina was in great shape, something he admired, but hiking was different than working out at the gym. He wondered if she was tired, and that was the reason for this spat.

"Stupid mosquitos."

"If we get going, then we can leave those behind too."

The stump and the moss showed where she'd slid on them. The rustling behind them diminished, and Jared breathed out in relief. At least he wasn't going to have to try and fight off some fanged beast.

"See that?" He gestured to the distance. "The thing left. It might have been a deer, and more scared of us than we were of it."

"Whatever you say." She was quiet, and then her attention went to a slender tree behind Jared. He turned to study it, but it was nothing more than a maple, struggling to get a foothold in this old growth forest. It didn't stand a chance against trees that had been there for centuries.

"Let's go." He longed to shake her to get her to do something. "We're going to lose the light soon."

They started to walk toward the campground. Five minutes, maybe ten, and they would be around friendly faces. The quiet was creeping him out.

She halted so fast that he was several steps ahead of her before he realized it. The area was thick with leaves, both those fallen in recent months, and those from prior years. His feet sunk in layers of them before they hit solid ground.

"Why are we stopping?" His exasperation showed, but he couldn't stop it.

She gave him what he would have said was a coy glance a few days ago. "There are many types of dryads, did you know that?"

He stared at her, the words not making sense. Carina set the pack down. He could almost see the campground through the trees. The branches closed, leaving the hint of artificial light behind.

"What the fuck are you talking about? We're losing valuable time. We have to get our tent up, and the food put away. Come on. You wanted a bathroom earlier, now is your chance."

A branch from the nearby tree reached down and brushed her cheek.

It was wind.

It had to be wind.

"I like the woods. The woods are my home."

The entire area was still, not even a bird making a sound.

"You hate them. You had no desire to come on this trip."

She pressed a palm to the trunk of a nearby oak that soared toward the sky. The thing was so tall he couldn't see the top of its branches, but was sure that the canopy reached hundreds of feet above them.

"That's what I told you, so you would insist. I learned something about you in the last weeks. You love a challenge. I needed a way to lure you into these woods." She raised her voice, and mimicked her side of their conversation from last week. "I'm not convinced. Are you sure you can keep me safe? Well, okay, if you think it will be fun."

He stared at her as she leaned against the massive tree. The branches rustled as if they were speaking.

Carina's smile was broad, but held no warmth.

"Then why?"

She levered herself away from the tree, after caressing its rough bark one last time. He reflected on what she said. *Dryad? Like the women he was just thinking about*?

"The woods are beautiful." She went to the next tree, and caressed it as well. Had the tree nearest to her moved? Jared was imagining this entire thing. He'd never had nightmares about trees before, but there was always a first time.

And a last one.

"Yeah, yeah, gorgeous. Let's go."

He measured the distance from himself to the invisible camp. If he high stepped it, he could be there in no time at all. He should just go. Carina could follow, or not, as she chose.

"They are magnificent, and the trees magical. Don't you agree?"

"If you say so." Arguing would get him nowhere.

An owl hooted, and Jared started. He hadn't noted the quiet, but when the bird made noise, he realized how hushed the entire area was. The leaves were acting as a blanket, and everything else in between was still.

"As I was saying—about dryads. Some are tied to the trees. Some can move around in the human world."

He snorted, the sound turning into a scoff. "Very funny, Carina. If you're trying to tell me you're a tree, I'll admit it's hilarious."

"Oh, Jared, you have no idea." Carina spoke words in a language he didn't understand.

"Whatever." He was out of here. "I'm going. You can stay here and commune with the fucking trees." All thoughts of marshmallows over the fire were gone.

He turned away, and smacked into a tree that he would swear hadn't been there a moment ago. He backed away, wild-eyed. Jared started to run, not caring which way he went. He blundered through leaves, branches, and over who knew what.

The trees pressed around him, tripping him with their roots. Jared slipped and fell, tumbling to the forest floor.

Tendrils encircled him, trapping his limbs, and spreading his body wide. His pack still hung from his back, the straps tugging him down. Jared's body was raised up, and he howled in panic. A branch snaked over his mouth, covering it with a leaf. Jared tried to bite through it, but the veins resisted his efforts.

"There, there," Carina said, reverting to English from whatever she'd been speaking. "Stop fighting, and it won't be so bad."

"Help," he cried, but the sounds came out muddled.

Carina gestured around them, from the nearest tree to the sliver of sky above.

"This used to stretch to the horizon, and beyond. Man keeps coming and taking pieces of us. Now it is diminished, and its power faded."

A branch came out of her jacket. It twined around her neck, not like a noose, but a limb.

"The forest must continue, and for that we require a sacrifice. I was the logical choice to find one because I'm a Hamadryad, and can move freely. Don't bother to ask. It's not important for you to understand. We don't do this out of malice. In order for the trees to survive, we need blood."

He kicked and clawed, but he couldn't break free of the tree's hold. The last thing Jared saw was a bark pattern that might have been a face. He strove to scream, but he had no voice. He struggled to fight back, but had no power. The trees crowded around him, lashing out with their branches. He twisted, howling under his leaf gag, but he couldn't escape.

After a time, he was still, staring toward the canopy. His fading mind strove to hold onto life before he gave up the fight, and breathed his last. Carina patted his face, and then turned away.

Then he thought nothing more.

The Weeds Grow Strong, Their Wordroots Deep

L. P. Melling

Ana steps from the shade of the weed-strangled wordtree. The child chews its fruit in glorious sunshine, her tongue drenched in lexicon. Diphthongs roll deliciously around her mouth like marbles. The berries burst with assonance. Sweet, succulent vowels with a tart consonant rind, soaked in knowledge and nourishment for the soul.

Across patches of bone-white earth and ink-black roots, Ana's friend Noam struggles to pick fruit from a sagging branch. His night-dark hair sticks up at angles like tangled roots, his leg knotted as a storm-bent bough.

Closing her eyes, the sun's warmth on her face, Ana licks up the fruit's alliterative allure from her fingers. She takes a bite of another berry, but it tastes bitter. Sticks in her throat as she swallows the new word.

Spitting out the pulp, Ana spots Noam close to another wordtree, one bearing false fruit.

"Noam, c'mon! We've taken too much," Ana calls, and brushes a ringlet of coffee-colored hair behind her ear. In the corner of her eye, she notices the slang-weeds tightening around the wordtree's trunk and feels regretful, sorry for the threatened nymforest her father tries to protect, and wishes she could help.

Noam's crooked leg dust-clouds as it drags behind him. He wipes the fruit juice from his mouth with his sleeve and takes Ana's offered hand: his palm warm and oily but comforting. His features pure innocence.

Once punctuated with blue-black flowers, the thinning nymforest is grammarless now, choked with slang-weeds. On the verge of being lost forever. They walk in silence until Noam snaps it like a rotten branch. "Ana... You think the false fruit can cure someone?"

"No. It's forbidden, Noam. Poisonous! The Elders told us."

"But, maybe—"

Ana's father, tribe leader, appears in the distance. Noam's hand slips free from her grasp. "Later, Ana."

"Okay. Later."

Face weary, Ana's father meets her, and kneels as if the nymforest's weight is resting on his shoulders. "What word did you learn today, little one?"

"Endangered." The word sticks in her teeth as she remembers the fruit's bitterness, its sickly taste.

Father nods dejectedly. He stares at her hard. "I hope you didn't take more than your fill."

Using all her will power, she imagines the clean taste of the word *truth*. "No, I swear!"

"So why are you sweating?"

A droplet falls from her brow onto the dusty earth. Ana holds her breath.

Father's stern face cracks into a smile. "It's okay, you're learning, child. But we must be careful. Now, let's get back before Mother hunts us both down," he says and winks at her.

They tread back home, Ana in her father's giant shadow, wanting to understand and unburden him. "How can we save the wordtrees, Father?"

"Doing what we've always done, darling. Plant more letter-seeds and saplings, spread the words through our stories. By not giving up hope," he says, and they fall quiet as the nym-forest.

* * *

At dusk, the narrative tribe gathers around the first wordtree that drips with the blood sun's last light. "The nym-forest's story is shrinking," the Elders say, "splintered to tinder and sapped words. The slang-weeds have taken root and will destroy everything we know and value."

* * *

The next day, Ana's hands are caked in soil and seed-letters when she finds Noam approaching the poisonous fruit. He plucks it from a low-hanging branch.

"Noam, don't!" she cries.

His henna eyes hopeful, he takes a bite and swallows hard , and his neck bulges as if it's stuck in his throat. Noam looks shocked as he digests what he's eaten, his expression frozen. He snaps out of his stupor and scrambles over to Ana. She thinks his leg is fixed at first, but it's knotted as ever. Breathlessly, he says, "The wordtrees aren't dying, Ana! They're . . . *adapting.*"

Noam falls. Ana casually helps him back up, careful not to bruise his pride further.

"I'm fine." He brushes himself down. "The fruit isn't poisonous, only truthful. The Elders can't accept the change." His tearful eyes lock onto a broken branch straight as a letter "I". Noam binds it to his leg with weeds. He rises, head held high, and strides forward.

Ana gasps. Her legs weak, she struggles to soak it all in. "I-I have to tell Father. The Elders have to know they've been wrong all this time." The forbidden fruit bears truth, she thinks, a seed of an idea to set Father free from his burden.

They walk home past weeds they thought spelled the nymforest's end. Wordtrees with non-indigenous germinations, loaned branches, flexible grammar-structures, and hybridized wordfruits.

On the threshold of their village, Ana notices a budded shoot and a change takes root inside her. Her mouth waters at the thought of new words, of nourishing wisdom. Heart swelling, she senses new stories growing around her.

Mehlman's Revenge

Christopher Ryan

Mehlman sneered. Nothing new for him. What else could you do in a world full of jerks? And there were none bigger than the family next-door. Always laughing like mental patients. Taking the garbage out in the morning of pick-up when he was trying to sleep instead of the evening before like decent human beings. Having barbecues in the backyard 'til as late as 9 o'clock or, on the weekends, even 10. Horrible people.

And he was determined to get rid of them.

But he couldn't do it himself. That frustrated the hell out of Mehlman. He tried wedging nails against the tires of their cars, and they'd gotten a few flats, but nothing really damaging. Then one of the useless sons caught him red-handed. The father didn't even kick his ass so Mehlman could sue, damn him. Instead, he lodged a legal complaint with the town, not asking for a penny, but making it an official record so if Mehlman did anything else to them, both actions would demonstrate a pattern of abuse, and he'd have to pay loads, maybe even do time. Bastard even agreed not to say a word to Mehlman's wife Marge. Probably loved the humiliation and how Mehlman was forced to be nice. He couldn't let that mortification stand.

So, he sneered and bided his time, waiting for the perfect idea. Months passed. Years. He didn't think of anything that couldn't come back to bite him in the ass. But then his son, actually Marge's son, a short, fat science nerd, finally proved useful.

He and Marge had tried diligently for years to have their own kids, but it never happened. Seeing those punks next door going to school every day. Or riding around the town on bicycles with their pack of friends. Or wandering off to college and then coming back home, all while their parents drove the same crappy sedans. That showed Mehlman how lucky he had been. Their struggle made him laugh every time he climbed into his muscle car, glad he was never saddled with the same burdens.

Sometimes life just works out.

Marge's dweeb, RJ, was some sort of plant scientist. A "progressive environmental bioengineer" he called himself, telling Mehlman one time after a few drinks that he spent his life developing plant hybrids or something for business and possible military use. Like the army needed assault gardenias.

Honestly, RJ had probably explained it better but who could bother to listen? Until he mentioned his latest project.

Turned out the crafty little drip was developing some kind of "aggressive" moss. Over Easter dinner, he bored the hell out of everybody talking about "multiple, diverse applications," claiming the moss would be able to replicate rapidly, and eat through weeds, fungus, or any harmful, naturally occurring growth. "For example," he droned on, "the mold that sometimes further damages property after these horrendous climate change-induced storms we've been having."

Yeah, he was a liberal idiot.

But his politics didn't make any difference, not once it dawned on Mehlman that those jerks next-door loved their lawn. One of their no good grown-ass kids worked on it all the time, doing everything Mehlman paid some company a pile of cash to do just so Marge wouldn't complain.

If that lawn was something they enjoyed, he wanted to destroy it.

Mehlman figured that all he needed to do was somehow get a little bit of RJ's miracle growth. How the hell was he going to do that? The geek had to keep the project at some lab, right? Mehlman knew he couldn't just drop in for a visit, especially since he didn't even know where tubby worked. It scorched his shorts to think this was the end of his revenge dreams. Turned out his plans were only ruined for a few annoying months.

Sometimes life just works out.

Marge had offered to cook Thanksgiving dinner, but the little science nerd had conned some desperate gold digger into marrying him. She had popped out a little brat that was something like six months old, and the disgustingly delighted new parents wanted to stay home for the baby's first TurkeyFest, so he and Marge had to go to them. Still didn't seem like any kind a big break for Mehlman until they got there and, over drinks, Plant-Man offered to show Mehlman his home lab.

"I get to monitor and work on my projects right here," RJ said with pride. "Admin would never have even considered it before Covid."

This guy was a bigger bore than Mehlman thought, but it was worth a shot. "What do you have back there?"

The brainiac rattled off all sorts of gibberish until he said, "Moss."

"Yeah, let's go see your stuff," Mehlman said. And he suffered through every other bit of botanical bull just to get near RJ's attack growth.

"How does this stuff work?"

"It feeds on what it is introduced to," RJ explained. "Theoretically, at least."

"How did you get it to survive from the lab to home?"

"This is the sturdiest life form I've ever worked with. These sample containers performed perfectly. Well, for the moss they did; my cannabis buds all died in transit."

"Bummer," Mehlman mocked, studying the green mess. "But how would this stuff work, um, in the field, uh, theoretically?"

"The working concept is to just spread a bit on whatever aggressive growth you want to get rid of and the moss eats and grows. Simple as that. The catch, however, is you have to make sure it can be restricted to its purpose. You don't want it wiping out an entire forest just to get rid of some poison oak."

"Fascinating." But Mehlman wanted exactly that. He dreamed of RJ's little beastie eating his neighbors' lawn, trees, house. Maybe he could get some on the dog to shut that thing up, too. All he had to do now was distract the schmuck.

Mehlman took what happened next as a sign from God or whomever the hell ran this whole mess. RJ's ugly baby started crying. He apologized, said he'd be right back, and ran off. Sometimes life just...

Mehlman grabbed one of RJ's little travel things, removed the top, spooned out a little bit of the miracle moss into the container, screwed the cover on tight and slid it into his pocket. "Happy Thanksgiving to me," Mehlman thought, moving to re-join the festivities, very pleased with himself.

* * *

It wasn't that cold yet when Mehlman snuck out to the edge of the neighbors' front lawn the next day. Those asshats had piled into one of their junkers and drove off somewhere. He looked around to make sure no one was watching, opened up his little vessel, and spilled the moss onto their grass, chuckling all the way back to his house.

He didn't see any progress for a couple of days. And then he noticed that the green stuff had somehow made its way into a crack in the dork family's driveway. And it was spreading. Good enough for him. He figured if it was working in one direction, it must be spreading in all directions, and that meant it was infiltrating their lawn. By next spring the schmucks will be spending a boatload of cash to get their lawn repaired.

Mehlman didn't sneer that whole afternoon.

As the days crawled unmercifully towards Christmas, he noticed the moss filling in the crack, moving towards his house. He knew that he had solid cement along the edge of his property and was sure that would block it, maybe even turn it around, so he wasn't worried. The next few days were rainy. He stayed in and watched the sports channels and football on Sunday, grumbling about how those lazy, rich bums just sucked all the fun out of the sport. He enjoyed cocktails at night with Marge and let nature take its course with the neighbors' lawn.

A few days later, he finally wandered outside hoping to see RJ's monster eating up the neighbors' happiness. Instead, something odd was going on with his own lawn. The damn moss had climbed right over his cement edging and started spreading itself across his property. He wasted good money on the damn landscapers to keep it all satisfactorily beautiful for Marge. If she saw this, she was going to be pissed, and that always cost him a bundle.

He waited until his wife went shopping and got out his long-unused gardening equipment. He dug up shovels full of that moss and tossed it over to the neighbors' yard when no one was looking, careful to get it all. Then he sprayed weedkiller over his lawn to keep it from coming back. He'd blame the landscapers for the lawn's condition. Let Marge loose on them. The old girl could still tear into people when she got angry.

"Don't mess with the king," he said to the relocated slop.

The next day the moss was... back. Like it took being dug up personally. Now it was halfway across the yard, touching the front steps. When he looked behind his bushes it was attaching itself to the basement window. How could it grow so fast? Get so far? This was way too much for him to shovel without Marge stomping out and demanding an explanation. But Mehlman had an ace up his sleeve.

"Enjoy your final hours, you bastard," he sneered before going inside.

The weather chick he liked ogling confirmed that it was gonna snow something fierce overnight. Freezing temps and, potentially, blizzard conditions. That combination would kill it.

Mehlman wouldn't let himself sulk over taking the "L". Okay, the moss didn't work out. Who cared? He'd come up with something else in the New Year. He mixed up a couple of cocktails for the wife and himself and watched some college ball, pleased when the snowfall started.

Die, sucker.

The snow was a spectacular foot and a half deep by the time he woke up that next morning. And it was Christmas Eve Day, so everyone's travel plans would be ruined. Double win! They wouldn't have to go and see the grandbrat, so Mehlman could just sit back, make some cocktails and enjoy the holiday the way he liked it best—just the two of them.

Now Marge, she liked surprises, but was such a snoop she proved to be her own worst enemy. She would sneak around hunting for presents, and then be all disappointed if she found them all and there was nothing else on Christmas morning. Over the years, Mehlman had become a champ at hiding them. See, Marge said she didn't like going down in the basement, it spooked her, so that was his go-to place. He could hide all her loot down there without worry. The only catch was he'd have to get up before she did on Christmas morning, bring up the swag, and stick it under the damn tree before she knew any better.

Pain in the ass.

Still, it was always worth it when she'd make a fuss about the magic of the holiday and all that nonsense. Then he'd be all, "Ho ho ho, a job well done. Let's get Christmas morning mimosas!"

He almost blew it this year. Woke up and Marge wasn't next to him. Then he saw the light glowing under the bathroom door. One of the blessings of aging, he thought, tiptoeing out. He crept down to the basement not bothering to turn on the light in case she noticed on her way back to bed.

At the bottom of the steps, he slipped and almost fell on his ass. He regained his balance, but the inside of his slipper was wet now, right through to his thick white sock. He hated that. Mehlman hit the flashlight app on his cell phone and nearly caught a heart attack right there.

It looked like Astroturf under his feet. And all across the basement floor. And on the walls, coming down from the front window.

He pulled his foot out of the muck, and slipped and slid his way over to the light switch. Had to struggle against the damned stuff to flip it.

The light went on.

Everything was green and gross and seemed to be trembling.

Nah. That wasn't quite it.

This stuff wasn't quivering.

It was moving.

Toward him.

He turned to run up the stairs but the moss had him by the ankles and was climbing its slimy way up his calves and under his pajamas, pulling at his bottoms, yanking them down, leaving his wrinkly butt hanging out. That's when he started to panic. It was crawling up his legs to his... other stuff.

He broke when he felt it enter his anus. Screamed for Marge.

A muffled cry turned his head.

Behind him, entirely covered, except for one horrified blue eye and a right hand holding one of her hidden presents, was Marge.

Mehlman tried to shriek but his mouth filled, killing all sound as the moss took him down.

The Soul of a Tree

Donna J. W. Munro

The wind rustled through the branches of the four-hundred-year-old oak, called Tamir, and his nearest brethren. Together they tangled on the green belt of the space, wide trunks sturdy in any storm, roots deep in the ground. Throughout his life, Tamir had flourished with the greatest trees, cloistered in a cluster that grew up together as he had hundreds of years before.

There used to be so many more trees, old like him.

Through the touching of roots, he could hear them telegraphing their thoughts, growing into a twined embrace in the soft peat and silt beneath them. He'd been just a youth then, some twenty and others thirty years old, when the wall grew up around him. Enclosed him and his nearest brethren inside, though his roots still touched the others outside the enclosure.

All along their connections, the trees grumbled of what they felt and imagined.

There were fewer trees. Fewer mind touches between the seeking tendrils of root.

Fewer roots.

Those he touched outside the wall no longer contemplated the skies and the movements of the stars. Instead, they worried about the sudden falling of brethren, about their death screams. that every tree-touching-root wept over.

Then he noticed the gaps in their green canopy.

Outside the wall, other things grew like saplings: first squat under the branches of a juvenile, then they'd be replaced by taller, sturdier things. Things wide and tall, though not like the mountains his distant cousin, the Joshua trees, once described. White like birch, tops thatched with straw. So quickly they popped up, he wondered what type of being they were. They had no roots. They made no sound unless they fell, and, even then, they didn't keen like a dying tree. Their death rattle was just a whispered sigh.

Inside the enclosure wall, he and his nearest brethren thrived. The green around them flourished. The sun smiled, and water quenched their thirst. All within the wall grew, but the conversations from outside of the enclosure ceased.

Tamir wished they hadn't given up their feet so long ago—to burrow down into the living soil that cradled them. If his people still had feet, they could go looking for the lost voices: Zamar the tall, greatest seer of the stars; Monatha, mother of many and a wonderful storyteller; Kotu, his favorite for her beautiful singing. How he longed to hear her voice again through the nest of his roots. Longed to touch her with his thoughts.

Together inside the enclosure wall, he and his brethren wondered if all those elder trees beyond the wall had been moved by some kind of new creatures. Where would they have taken the others?

Tamir and his brethren wanted to act, but cut off from the wisdom of the others, they were blind. They dared not guess at their fates.

Looking toward the wall surrounding him and over the top, so few of the old ones still stood. He'd look one moment and they'd be there, then the next, they'd be gone, their keening bellow blasting through the soil where there weren't even roots for the thoughts to travel along.

Tamir, a naturalist tree, tended to look down at the soil, rather than up at the sky, or inward like most of his kind. He'd made discoveries during his long life. Tiny creatures, invisible to the naked eye, flashed through their branches. He'd only seen them through the magnifying filter of rain, but he'd found them and made his name among the others. Once he'd identified the tiny things, the others looked for themselves. Sometimes the little things would die upon a branch and settle there long enough to be studied. Harmless little things.

He knew the other brethren couldn't be harmed by fur or wings.

"Once you know about the hidden world within hollows and bark," he'd lectured for the others in the root web, "you cannot unsee the depth of life around you."

Then came the death of many over the last hundred years.

He thought long on it, consulting with others and studying the growth of the block things outside the wall—tall, shiny, and loud. A solid din of screeching with a banging that fluttered across his understanding. There had to be another thing responsible. Something small and fast. Something they'd never considered. The trees understood creeping sickness and disease. Even the stoutest among them might splinter under the yeasty spot disease's bite. He studied, turning his eyes low, watching the things growing between his roots.

"Watch out," bellowed his rootmate.

A storm from above—so quick in his eye that all he saw was the flash of it—struck him, cutting into his canopy with a deafening crack. So fast and his outside peeled away, large branches of him crashing to the ground. Time slowed for him as his heart-sap thickened, and his brethren waited for his keening death. But the parts the sky fire hadn't hit lived and felt strong. He'd never again fill the sky as he had, but he'd live on another thousand years.

The root nest glowed with happiness.

But he noticed streaks of light zipping around his fallen parts. Dashing bits of sound buzzing. The pieces disappeared. Something was eating his dead flesh. Something that moved so much faster than him. He cried out to the roots that he'd found a new creature, something so fast it couldn't be seen. Something that moved like fire from the sky and that ate trees.

Tamir roared, "Brethren, that is where our friends have gone."

But the others scoffed. His injury must have affected his rationality. There was no evidence for little light monsters.

That's when the pain bit into his side, savage as the sky fire. It ripped him—his glorious trunk, the wondrous canopy that fed him, all the growth he'd made in his life— fell to the green. All he was, gone. In the moments he keened, roots shrinking back from the others as his connection to the brethren died, he saw the lights slow until he saw them.

Things on feet. Things that hadn't given up movement for thought.

Monsters chewing through his flesh and spitting it out in shreds. All he was, gone.

So he keened his sadness into the soil, alone and low.

* * *

"Hated to bring it down, but the city didn't like how it looked after that lightning hit," Joe said.

"Yeah, ugly old thing," Ronnie said, feeding the branches into the mulcher.

"Three hundred, maybe four hundred years old. Wonder what all it saw in those years, ya know?"

"Trees don't see, asshole. They got no eyes."

Joe nodded, still sad about the whole thing. He cranked up the stump grinder and started his work.

Always Alone

Diane Arrelle

Megan walked home alone.

It was a long walk through the forest, but Megan didn't mind. She liked the solitude, the sounds of autumn as the wind gently rustled the leaves in the trees and the foliage crunched under her feet, giving off a musky, slightly spicy odor.

She walked between the trees, then turned left toward the strange circle where nothing seemed to grow. The other kids in her eighth-grade class told her the space was haunted.

Megan walked into the circle and found it creepy and cold. She could swear she heard voices calling out to her.

Shivering as a chill rushed down her spine, Megan walked a little faster than her normal pace. As soon as she cleared the bare patch, she bolted through the final few dozen yards of trees to her backyard.

Ella, her cat, was sitting on a tree stump licking her paw, as if she knew Megan would come bursting through the forest at any moment.

Megan ran to the cat and swooped her up into her arms as she rushed into the house.

"Megan? Is that you?" her mother called from the kitchen. "You're late."

"I walked."

"Megan," her mother scolded. "I've told you before not to walk along the main road. It is deserted and dangerous."

Megan sighed, feeling a mixture of frustration and total annoyance, "I didn't use the road, I walked through the woods."

"My God, that's even worse!" her mother yelled. "Why didn't you take the bus?"

"Cuz."

"Because what?"

"Cuz, I can't stand it here. All the kids are just jerks who spend their time making fun of me."

"Making fun of you? Who is picking on you now? Megan, we moved so you'd get away from those so-called friends you had back home. I think it is time for you to make an effort to find some nice kids to hang out with and to get rid of that chip on your shoulder!"

"Oh, go to Hell!" Megan screamed. "I hate you, I hate this place, I hate my entire life." She turned and ran outside, back through the woods, back to that place where nothing grew, back to that place surrounded by bent, gnarled Halloween trees. She plopped down on the cold, damp, dead leaves that covered the ground and wept. How was she ever going to survive living in a town like this? She couldn't wait to turn sixteen so she could drop out of school and quit having to pretend she cared about anyone else. She thought about running away. Even living on the streets of the city had to be better than barely existing out here in the middle of nowhere.

She looked up and thought she'd heard voices agreeing with her. "Yessss," whispered through the leaves.

She got up and studied the trees. She touched the thick, rough, grayish bark that seemed to have patterns in the ridges. Some even looked like faces—faces with mouths opened in frozen screams. Suddenly, the wind howled through the clearing, causing the leaves to violently swirl around her like she was in the middle of a mini tornado.

The bark grew hot to her fingers as the wind chilled her all the way through.

Her feet suddenly seemed rooted to the ground, but with a sharp tug she broke free and ran back home.

***

A few days later, she walked home from school and several of the girls from her class followed her. “Hey, Megan,” the one named Bethany called. “Wait up, we want to talk to you.”

Megan kept walking. She could hear the girls behind her calling and giggling. Then she heard their pounding footsteps as they ran to catch up. They walked alongside her, seemingly unaware that she was totally ignoring them.

“So, Megan.” Bethany said. “We see you walking through here every day. Don’t you know these woods are haunted? Don’t you know that people have disappeared in these woods, never to be heard from again?”

Megan muttered just loud enough to be heard, “Well, maybe we’ll get lucky today and you guys will just vanish.”

The girls giggled again. “Seriously, Meg, you ought to not walk home this way,” the short blond one, Rachel added. “It’s true about the disappearances. Why, my mother’s cousin vanished one Halloween when she was trick or treating. My mother and all her cousins have told me about it.”

Megan rolled her eyes. “Oh, just give me a break. I’m not a stupid kid from the suburbs you know. I don’t fall for any of that horror garbage. Go find another new kid to scare. I’m not afraid of anything, especially hick stories from a town of losers.”

“Well, we were just trying to be friendly,” Bethany snapped. “Besides, you are the only new kid around.”

“Yeah,” the third girl, Sara piped in. “And you’re always acting like such a bitch.”

Bethany glared at Sara, “Look Megan, it’s Halloween tonight and we thought we’d give you one more chance. We were going to ask you to join us for the Halloween Bonfire Party at the lake.”

Megan turned to face the three girls. "Another chance? For what, to be your friend? Look, no thanks. Why don't you leave me alone!"

The other girls stepped back a bit. They started to turn away when Bethany signaled them to stop. "OK, you think we are just a bunch of hicks who make up stories. Why don't you just prove how brave you are, I dare you to come out to the dead place at the stroke of midnight. We'll meet you there and if you don't chicken out, we'll never bother you again."

"You got a deal," Megan said as she turned her back on the girls and walked home.

After dinner she went to her room and locked the door. At eleven o'clock she called to her mother that she was going to bed. At eleven forty-five she opened her bedroom window and crept out. As she hit the ground, something hit her in the legs. Megan fought to keep her balance, and fought to keep her wits. What had attacked her? She looked down, pointing the beam of her flashlight into a pair of glowing eyes. The breath caught in her throat until Ella rubbed against her legs and meowed.

Megan blew her breath out and laughed. "Damn, Ella, you scared me."

She stood up and flashed her light into the trees. The forest was thick and black, but Megan had a point to prove. She figured those girls were going to chicken out, but she was going through with it. Just in case. And besides, she wanted to prove to herself that she was tough enough to face anything on her own.

Alone.

As she carefully wove her way between the trees, the woods were dead quiet. Almost too quiet. There was no wind, no animal sounds, only her own footsteps. Ella followed, then ran ahead. Megan neared the clearing where nothing grew. She swept her light beam around and saw that someone had swept the leaves out of the middle and into piles all around the circle. As Megan neared a pile, Ella screeched and hugged against Megan's legs.

She bent to pick up the cat, but the wind kicked up and the cat arched its back in terror. Ella ran straight into the nearest pile of leaves just as the wind made them swirl upwards into a wild dance of forbidding shadows. Megan couldn't hear anything over the howling wind and the rustling, crunching of the dried leaves.

She called out, "Ella!" but the cat was lost to her in the swirling, twirling, dancing leaves.

Then as if nothing had just happened, the leaves fell back into their piles and all was calm. Megan flashed her light all around. "Ella?" she called.

Nothing. No cat. No answering meow. Just darkness and silence. And the tiniest sound of crying, so soft Megan wasn't sure she'd heard it at all.

"Ella?" Megan called again. She listened hard, straining to hear something. Suddenly she heard a soft, sad mewing.

"ELLA!" Megan shouted, fighting off a feeling of dread in her stomach. "Ella, where are you?"

As if in answer, the moon cleared the clouds and the woods became streaked with shades of gray. Megan listened to the cat's muffled cries and wildly wove her beam every which way. Then she saw it, on the side of one of the gnarled trees. In the bark!

Megan screamed, tears coursing down her cheeks. She went up to the tree and with a shaky, tentative hand reached out to the rough gray bark. The shape of the whorls were still moving but as her hand rested on the hot wood, her fingers traced the shape of a cat. A cat caught in mid-yowl. "Ella," Megan whispered, then began to back away into the middle of the dead circle. "Oh, Ella!"

The cat shaped swirls in the bark stopped moving, solidifying into an eternal pattern and Megan heard a final, sad, pained cry. As if in answer to the cat's forlorn yell, the wind picked up again and the trees began to sway with a violent, rocking motion. Megan turned the light on them and shuddered as they bent toward her, forcing her to the very center of the circle. She couldn't move in any direction, the leaves swirled around and around getting closer to her with every breath. Megan spun around, trying to find a break, but the swaying branches beat at her, keeping her centered. The leaves swirled higher and spun faster and faster until all the leaves from all the piles that had surrounded the circle formed a spinning wall. Megan screamed and pushed at the branches. She tried to beat her way out, but the leaves closed in.

Megan was caught in a maelstrom of crunching brown that reeked of musk and spice. It was overpowering: she couldn't breathe, she couldn't speak, she couldn't move. Suddenly she realized she was frozen in place.

She was paralyzed, but she found her voice. "Help me," she screamed as the leaves settled once again on the barren floor of the clearing. Megan realized she had somehow been moved by that leaf cyclone, forced over to the ring of trees. She struggled to move her arms and her legs, to take a deep breath, but she couldn't move. Even her eyes were frozen in position.

She tried to stay calm.

She waited. After what seemed like forever, she heard voices. It was the girls and they brought some friends along. *Oh good, help is coming*, Megan thought.

There had to be a dozen kids shining flashlights all around. Megan heard laughter. "I knew she was full of it," Bethany giggled. "A big-mouth coward."

"Yeah," Sara agreed. "I knew she'd chicken out. Her kind always does."

"Help," Megan called. "Help me; I'm trapped inside this tree!"

Bethany spun her light around. "Did you hear that?"

"What?" someone asked.

Bethany shrugged. "Nothing, I thought I heard her calling."

"I didn't hear anything," chorused around the group.

"Come on," one of the kids yelled. "It's cold out here. Bet that Megan won't show her face in school tomorrow."

The rest laughed their agreement.

"No! Wait!" Megan screamed as the kids started to leave. "Bethany, Bethany, help me!"

Bethany stopped and shone her light around the circle one more time. "Didn't you hear that? She called my name."

"Bethany, you're nuts," one of the kids said and pushed her out of the clearing.

Megan was left alone in the dark. Really alone.

It was what she had always wanted. Only, she realized too late, not this way. She saw the other faces in all the other trees and realized that she was as she had always been, alone in a crowd.

Into the Deep Forest

DJ Tyrer

"Sorry, tell me again why we're here and not on a beach or surfing or whatever?" Todd asked as he climbed out of the battered, old, yellow jeep and swiped at something large that buzzed past his head.

Kimo laughed. "Seriously? Hawaii isn't just beaches, man, or hadn't you noticed what was in front of you as you surfed back to shore?" He gestured around at the lush tangle of plant-life that rose over the trail. "This island has some phenomenal scenery—remember the waterfall in Jurassic Park? Heck, I could name a dozen films."

"Yeah, sure, but . . ." Todd shrugged. "This was supposed to be a holiday."

"And?"

"And, tramping miles isn't my idea of a fun holiday."

"You haven't gone two feet, yet." Kimo patted the side of the jeep. "We'll take it nice and slow and I guarantee you'll see some real wonders. Things that will outdo even the most lovely sea view—I guarantee it."

"They better."

"Hey, it comes with my money-back guarantee." He laughed, again.

Todd rolled his eyes. He wasn't paying Kimo a cent, unless you counted bar bills. They'd hit it off in a bar and Kimo had said he'd show him the sights. Already, he'd taken Todd to a reconstruction of an ancient Hawaiian village and up Mauna Loa.

"Follow me, man." Kimo set off along the faintest hint of a dirt track between the trees and Todd hurried after him.

"Is it safe?"

"The islands are free of dangerous predators. You might see some wild cattle—but, they're only dangerous if you drive into them. Worst thing likely to happen out here is you trip over a root and twist an ankle. So, keep your eyes peeled."

Kimo grinned.

As they walked, he would gesture at the trees and other plants and provide a commentary.

Todd sighed. "Uh, as fascinating as all this is, I'm really not in the mood for a nature ramble. Are we going to see anything cool?"

"There's an amazing waterfall up ahead. Maybe ten minutes away."

"It better be amazing."

"It is. It—" Kimo halted, suddenly.

Todd almost walked into the back of him.

"What is it?" he asked, steadying himself.

Kimo didn't answer, so Todd looked over his shoulder.

A coconut sat on the path before them.

"Earth to Kimo, it's a coconut."

Kimo looked around. "Do you see a coconut tree around here?"

Todd shrugged. "Well, no."

"That's because you find coconuts down by the shore, not way up here."

"So? Somebody left a coconut."

"Yeah... I'm sure that's all it is... " Kimo shook himself. "We should go back."

Todd glanced at his cell. There was no signal, but it could still tell him the time.

"It's early," he said.

Kimo took a deep breath, then turned to face him.

"My grandfather was a kahuna."

"Isn't that a type of hamburger?" Todd waved away Kimo's splutter with a chuckle. "Yeah, I remember, from that village—a kahuna was an old-timey priest, right?"

"Exactly."

"So, what's that got to do with coconuts?"

"It's got everything to do with this particular coconut."

"Sorry, still not following you."

"Look, my grandfather told me all about the old ways. There used to be a shrine to the god Kū up here—Ku-olono-wao, Kū of the Deep Forest."

"And?"

"One of the forms that Kū can take is that of—"

"A coconut?" Todd interrupted him.

"Yeah." Kimo gave an embarrassed shrug.

"So, what? You're saying that coconut is some old Hawaiian god? Seriously? Oh, man... " He began to laugh.

"Well, when you put it like that... " Kimo shifted, awkwardly.

"It's probably just a coincidence. Or, maybe someone put it there as a joke or something."

He shoved past Kimo and gave it a kick.

"Ouch!" He reached down to rub his toes through his sneaker. "I guess that's Kū's revenge, eh?"

"You shouldn't mock."

"Look, it's just silly superstition. You're not seriously going to tell me you believe in all that old kook?"

"Well... no... " Kimo's tone was reluctant.

"So, let's go see that waterfall—and, it better be amazing."

"It is... "

Slowly, Kimo began to lead the way along the track, again, gradually picking up pace.

"So, this Kū—he's the god of the forest?"

"I don't want to talk about it."

"Come on, you started it. You've got me curious."

"Yeah, among other things."

"Like what?"

"War. Farming, Fishing. All sorts. Different, er, aspects. Like... "

"Like?"

"Ku-waha-ilo."

"Koo-wahoo-whatsit?"

Kimo shot him a look. "Don't mock."

Todd gave him a cheesy grin. "Would I?"

Then, he asked, "Anyway, Koo-whatever-you-said. What was he about?"

"Sorcery. It means 'Kū-of-the-maggot-dripping-mouth'."

"Lovely. And, here I thought Hawaii was all about sand, sea, surf and shirts. But, no, there are maggots, too. Wonderful."

"Look, let's change the tune, eh? We're nearly at the waterfall, okay?"

Ahead of them, the narrow track widened out into a clearing that led down to a large pool at the foot of a towering cliff decorated with splashes of greenery down which poured a scintillating waterfall. The lush greens and beautiful blue of the water looked almost artificial.

Todd couldn't help but gasp. "Amazing... "

A small, short-haired, brown-grey dog stood between them and the pool. Kimo stared at it.

"I thought you said these woods were devoid of dangerous predators," Todd said with a laugh.

He crouched down. "Here, boy."

"Don't," Kimo hissed at him.

"What on earth is it, now?"

"Another of the forms Kū could take was that of a dog... "

Todd sighed. "So, first a coconut, now a dog? Are you for real?"

He called the dog, again.

"I'm out of here," Kimo told him, backing away out of the clearing.

"Sure, whatever. I'll see you back at the jeep."

Kimo said something, but Todd didn't hear.

"Here, boy. Here, boy."

The dog trotted towards him and halted just in front of him, looking at him with wide, dark eyes.

Todd reached out to stroke it. The dog opened its mouth.

“Ah! Hell, no!”

A torrent of maggots flowed out of the dog’s mouth onto the ground before him.

“Hell, no!” Todd tried to scramble back and fell flat onto his butt, maggots piling up before him.

The writhing pile continued to grow unfeasibly high, hiding the dog from view.

Impossibly, the pile appeared to take on a shape, growing to look more and more like the figure of a man.

Todd couldn’t believe it. He screamed as it took a step towards him.

Somewhere, down the track, he was certain Kimo could hear his shrieks, but he knew the Hawaiian would never return for him. He’d been right and Todd should have heeded his warnings.

The impossible figure reached out for him.

There, in the forest’s heart, Kū would claim his first sacrifice in over a hundred years.

Voices in the Wind

Ann Stolinsky

"YOU LEAVE HIM ALONE!"

Spit from Grampa's mouth hit my hair, threatening to slide down my forehead. I wiped my face and hair with my left shirt sleeve.

Frantically I stepped back, almost losing my balance on the gravel road. Grampa grimaced as he bent to clutch my right hand. He shook his clenched fist in the air violently, his white knuckles pointing toward the woods.

"You can't have him! Leave him alone!"

Fearful, I pulled away, my bicycling feet the catalyst for loose gravel to pelt us. Arms outstretched, eyes wide, my heart pounding, I clawed Grampa's hand with my left hand, wanting to be released from his tight grip. I won free. I was frightened, both *for* my Grampa and *of* him.

Grampa's tone of voice and ferocity of his words scared me. I'd never heard him speak so forcefully. Releasing my hand brought his attention back to me. His crimson face scared me more than his tone. Grampa reached for my hand. Tears welled in my five-year-old eyes. Through my tears, I peered into the woods. I saw nothing but nature, birds and trees and insects. The tall trees silently announced the impending end of summer, their leaves turning various shades of yellows and oranges and reds, some already brown. I thought the woods were beautiful.

"Don't you let go, don't ever let go of my hand!" Grampa scolded as he grabbed me. Scooping me up in a tight embrace, he ran down the road, heading for home. My tears and snot drenched his favorite flannel shirt. I sniffed, the scents of Grampa's sweat and his fear filling my nostrils.

Home was a little shack, half-hidden by overgrown vines. Grampa ran through the broken gate in what was once a white picket fence, past the vegetable garden filled with swelling pumpkins, past the rocking chair on the crumbling porch.

Grampa sighed as he reached the screen door with its holey netting that let the summer heat and winter cold in freely. He always sighed before entering the house, and even his anger today didn't break the tradition. He'd look up at the roof, its missing shingles covered with plywood. Usually he'd tell me my Daddy had promised to fix the roof but didn't get around to it. Today Grampa sighed, but didn't speak. He grabbed the door and flung it open, entering the house in one fluid motion. The screen door banged shut.

"Grampa, who were you yelling at?" I asked when he finally put me down. My shoulders stopped heaving, and my breathing slowed as I calmed down. Grampa was weary from carrying me on the run. Veins on his forehead pulsed, and perspiration puddled in the valleys that were his wrinkles.

"Don't matter, boy. Don't you worry about it. Just you stay close to me when you're outside, you hear?"

"Grampa," I mumbled, my small voice quivering. My palms were moist and my tears almost spilled over again. "Grampa, did you see Daddy out there?"

Grampa sat down on his favorite chair, the one with the frayed brown tweed cover, before answering. "No, Sonny, I didn't see your Daddy. Your Daddy is gone, I told you that."

* * *

When I was ten, the school held a father-daughter dance. And then a mother-son dance. Grampa just looked at me and sighed when I asked him about my mother and father.

* * *

On my thirteenth birthday, Grampa took me shopping in town. I was allowed to pick out anything I wanted. We had read a book in school a couple of years back about a boy and a magic lamp that granted wishes. Grampa laughed, said he was my magic genie and would grant my wishes. I weighed my options carefully. Did I want a new bike, some candy or new video games? I told Grampa I needed to think about it, and we headed home.

* * *

After dinner Grampa snuggled into his chair to read the newspaper. His wrinkles had deepened, and his jowls hung where the elasticity of his skin had failed him. He looked old from years of hard work and tired from years of worry. White hair still covered his scalp, a sharp contrast to his sun-browned skin. Too old to sit on his lap, I pulled a chair next to his. He faced me, little lines appearing prominently at the ends of his smile. "Grampa," I began hesitantly, "I know what I want. Tell me about the day I was born. Tell me about my parents."

His smile disappeared, and his shoulders slumped, as if in defeat. Grampa sighed. "Sonny, you're getting older, and I guess it's time you knew. Bring me that picture from the table, you know the one." Holding the picture, his gnarled finger pointed to the tall man. "This picture is the last I have of your Daddy.

"Your Gramma and I were never blessed with a child of our own. When we were in our thirties, someone left an infant on our doorstep. We had no idea where he came from. Local authorities put out the word, asking if anyone had lost a child, but no one claimed the baby boy.

"We had been content to live childless, but when we saw that beautiful baby boy, swaddled in a blue blanket, our hearts opened. Nobody claimed him, so we were allowed to adopt him. We loved your daddy like he was born to us naturally. We took walks on the beach—

that's where we lived when he came to us. I still remember the sound of his laughter when the tide came in." Grampa paused to wipe his forehead, attempting to hide his tears from me. "He played in the surf and sand, making giant sand castles that threatened to reach the sky. We never could understand why, but he'd always populate his sand castles with the most interesting-looking creatures. He had a gift for making birds and butterflies and bugs out of wet sand. No people, just nature. Miniature trees surrounded his castles. Your daddy was very creative. His mind was always on the next sand castle, and how he could make it bigger and better.

"As your daddy grew, we'd still take walks together on the beach, and he'd still swim in the water, but there was something else in his life... a longing he couldn't explain. His eyes seemed to go deep into himself, and he grew distant. That's when *they* showed up." Grampa spat out the word *they*.

"One day, when your daddy was a teenager, we had a disagreement. I looked out the window to see him getting on his bicycle. He was off to a friend's house. He sat on the bike, his hair blowing in the wind, head cocked to the side, looking around, listening. Then talking. I don't know what he heard, or who he was talking to, but the expression on his face scared me. I ran outside, figuring my excuse for going out there would be my intention to apologize. He turned sharply when he heard me, and his glare was daggers. All he said was, 'Now they've gone. You should have stayed inside.'

"Your Gramma and me talked about what had happened. We were afraid whoever's baby he was would be coming for him. Your Gramma and me and your daddy moved the next day. We knew he couldn't stay there. We were afraid they'd take him from us.

"So, we moved here, figuring if we lived in a rundown shack near the woods no one's gonna find him."

Grampa bit his lip and asked me for a glass of water. He took a sip, then put it on the end table. He worried his fingers.

"Your daddy started to change that day. He had enhanced vision. He saw a hawk in the sky coming toward us from who knows how many miles away, but your Gramma and I didn't see it until several minutes after he did. And his night vision! At midnight, he could tell me how many leaves were on a tree across the road."

Grampa took another sip of water. His trembling hands betrayed him and he spilled a bit on his pants. Ignoring the spot, he went on.

"His hearing grew sharper. I could be talking to your Gramma in the kitchen with your daddy upstairs in the bedroom and he'd hear every word we said." Grampa smirked and laughed. "Not that he obeyed us any more than before. But we knew he heard us." Grampa sighed. "He became more distant, not sharing stories about school or friends with us anymore. He grew tall as the trees, and when he was old enough he went off to work. But he always came home to us, every night."

Grampa grabbed my hand. "Listen closely now, boy." I moved my chair closer, so my knee was touching his. Grampa nodded.

"The afternoon your daddy turned twenty-one, he went into the woods and didn't come back for twenty-four hours. Your Gramma and I were worried about him. He'd never done that before. When he came back, he brought us you. You were a little thing, just lost in your daddy's long arms and big hands. Red-faced and screaming, that was the first view we had of you. We fell in love with you instantly. Your daddy said you were his. His face was shining like only a new daddy's face can look. We believed him. We asked where's the baby's momma. Your daddy told us there wasn't a momma, and refused to talk about the subject further.

"We did the only thing we could do. We dug out your daddy's old crib from the attic and went to the store for some diapers and formula."

Grampa patted my hand.

"We believed your daddy would be a good father. After getting you settled into your new room, your daddy went outside to stare at the stars. Gramma and I left him be. We felt he could learn how to change a diaper the next day. He needed time to himself. An hour or so later your Gramma and I were feeding you when we heard your daddy screaming. 'No, you can't take me now! No, you can't have me! I want to raise my son!'

"By the time we ran down the steps and outside, holding you, there was no sign of him. He was gone. We heard a faint sound in the wind. It sounded like 'Aaron. I love you.' That's why we named you Aaron.

"Your Gramma died when you were a toddler. Do you remember her?"

I nodded, tears welling my eyes.

"She loved you, oh my how she loved you, but she pined for your daddy something fierce. I guess her heart was broken, losing her only son.

"Do you remember that day I screamed and scared you? You were five-years-old, a growing and curious boy. That day I saw a shadow in the woods, heard a faint voice in the wind. 'Aaron,' it sounded like." Grampa gripped my hand tighter. "I know you want to meet your daddy, but I can't lose you. If you go to him, I don't know what will happen to you. Or to me. Promise me you won't leave me. Promise me you won't listen to the voices in the wind."

That night I hugged Grampa tightly, his shoulders heaving, this time from tears and not from running scared. I promised Grampa I'd never leave him.

* * *

Grampa died this afternoon, on my twenty-first birthday. Sweat poured off my brow and stained my shirt as I put the last of the dirt on top of his grave. My shovel fell to the ground, unwilling to stay against the side of his beloved shack where I left it. I let the shovel lie where it fell. I won't be using it anymore.

I showered, and put on my best clothes. I packed a light supper, some cheese and crackers, a flask of water, enough for two. Hopefully my father will find me quickly when he hears my voice in the wind.

Tangled in the Tree of Ghosts

Tim Newton Anderson

Everyone knew about the Witch's Tree on our estate. When someone died tragically, a bunch of flowers, or a favorite toy would suddenly appear leaning against the trunk, joining the faded remnants of all the others that surrounded the dead tree.

The story everyone told in school was that the tree had been there for hundreds of years—long before the Longmeadow Estate had been built. It was the last tree of an ancient, sacred wood that had been chopped down to build the village of Meadowvale. Everyone said they used to hang witches from the tree, back in the days of the Witchfinder General.

My best friend was Billy Wilson. He was in my year and doing as well as I was, despite coming from a family that had always thought learning was a waste of time and earned their money doing seasonal work in the tourist industry or the odd bit of laboring. Like me, he rarely wore the branded trainers and shirts the rest of the class had. I had homemade or patched clothes that had been let out as I grew, and he wore cheap imitations that had been bought at a street market or had fallen off the back of a lorry.

It was Billy that first told me about the Witch Tree when we were in primary school, walking back home in the semi-dark of winter when its bare branches clawed at the sky like skeletal fingers.

He said the tree had grown from the body of a powerful witch who had been buried alive on the spot and the trunk and branches were a magical arm reaching out from her grave. One day, when she had grown strong enough, the wooden arm would grab the ground and pull the giant witch from the earth to take her revenge on the descendants of the people who had buried her.

Billy said at Halloween the witches would sneak out of their houses and dance naked around the dead tree, laying their curses on children who had annoyed them by playing knock down ginger or kicking footballs in their garden. Everyone knew who the witches were, Billy said. The old women who lived alone—normally with lots of cats. They would pretend to be nice and invite children in for biscuits, but no child dared take them up on their offer. Billy explained, "If you went into the witch's house, you would never come out. They would eat you or turn you into yet another cat. Even if you did come out, you would not be the same."

The children said that when the witches danced around the tree, the spirits of all the people they killed could be seen. They were tethered to the dead branches, waving in the wind like bizarrely shaped balloons. And their quiet cries would blend with the whistling of the wind—calling out to be set free from their eternal captivity.

I didn't believe in ghosts and witches, but perhaps the story was why people put flowers on the tree when someone died. It was an offering to the witches so they would let their relatives free and leave the rest of the family alone.

My friendship with Billy changed after his brother died. Well, to be honest, it was Billy that changed. He was always a bit "spacey" and would often be off in a dream, but he became even more quiet. I would talk to him and become aware he was no longer listening. He had loved to play football, but one day he just turned and walked off as the ball rolled past and on into the road. More and more he would just get up and leave to be somewhere by himself. He even did it in class sometimes—just standing up silently and walking out the door. The teachers didn't do anything at first because they knew he was hurting, but after he did it for the six or seventh time he was taken in to see the Headmistress. It didn't make any difference.

It was his oldest brother that had died—Nathan. Although there were a sister and another brother between them in age, it was Nathan that Billy always turned to if he was troubled. It was Nathan more than their parents who ran the family on a day-to-day basis—making sure all the kids were dressed, had breakfast, got to school, and came back at bedtime. It was Nathan who read to them as they fell asleep. Not that their mum and dad were unkind or didn't love them, they had just passed more and more responsibility onto Nathan as they got on with their lives.

The accident definitely wasn't his fault. He had been walking safely along the pavement when a car had swerved off the road. The driver was devastated—he had never had an accident in the twenty years he had been driving—and couldn't understand why his foot and hands had suddenly gone into spasm and veered into Nathan.

Billy, of course, blamed the witches. He started walking past the houses of the old women who were supposed to be members of the coven. He didn't do anything—just stood outside their gardens and stared in with glaring eyes—hoping to find a clue as to which of them was responsible for Nathan's death. Everyone was worried about him. The school managed to get one of the educational psychologists to come and talk to him, but he had one of his "normal" moods when they did their tests and he was passed as being okay. And most of the time he was. It was only when those strange moods suddenly descended that he would cut himself off from everyone and stand in mute contemplation outside someone's house, hoping to catch a glimpse through the net curtains of something that would explain why his brother had been taken from him so suddenly.

So I wasn't surprised when I heard a tap on my bedroom window late on Halloween and looked out to see Billy standing in the street below, beckoning me to come and join him.

I loved Halloween. I got what would normally be a year's worth of sweets in one night. It wasn't scary. You were probably safer than most other nights because everyone knew there would be groups of kids going from door to door and looked out for them. But at half past eleven the streets were empty. It had been a clear night earlier, but now a thin high cloud covered the sky and the moon was just a smudge of light. There were a few tendrils of mist creeping across the road like a nervous cat and climbing the trees to find safety among the bare branches.

I quickly put some warm clothes on and sneaked down the stairs and out the back door.

"I'm going to go to the Witch Tree to see if Nathan is there," he said. "This is the night he should appear. I'm going to try and make the witches set him free."

I don't mind admitting a chill of fear ran through me and settled like a block of ice in my stomach. It was bad enough being out in the dark at this time of night, without going to the spookiest place on the estate, but I could see Billy was determined.

It was the quiet that was most scary. As we walked towards the witch tree there was no sound except the soft slap of our trainers on the pavement slabs, the beating of my heart, and shallow breathing. Billy had said his piece and was walking in silence with a determined look on his face. I was sure he was as scared as me, but his sense of purpose was driving him on.

I don't really know what Billy expected to see at the Witch Tree. There were lots of stories—naked women dancing, goats, devils, giant cats, and who knows what else, but I didn't really think there would be anything there at all.

I saw the tree surrounded by swirls of mist, but Billy clearly saw something else.

"It's covered in a whirlwind of ghosts," he said, staring with wild eyes. "I can see through them—they're pale grey. I can make out the heads and shoulders but their legs are more like tails, or those long filmy dresses women wear in films for dances or posh parties."

He pulled his eyes away from the tree for a second and looked at me with an expression of awe.

"Nathan took me to a trout farm once and the water exploded with fish when you put some food in. The ghosts are dancing just like that in the air. It's marvelous and terrifying at the same time."

Despite the warm clothing I had put on, my teeth were chattering. All I could see was the mist curling through the branches. Billy had lost it. His grief had tipped him over the edge.

He was rooted to the spot, watching what he imagined was the dance of the ghosts around the dead tree.

"I can make out some of the faces," he said. "I can recognize the old man found dead after they noticed all the milk bottles on the step. And the lady my mum had said died from cancer a year ago. And the woman who killed herself after her baby died—she's still holding her dead daughter to her chest."

He suddenly started to cry.

"It's Nathan. In amongst them. He doesn't see me. Just a blank look. No horror, or fear, or anger, but like he's totally lost hope."

I was frozen in place, but Billy ran forward and stood at the base of the tree, shouting his brother's name. Whenever he imagined Nathan close enough to the ground, Billy would jump up and try to touch him, hands passing through the mist. My heart went out. He thought he had found Nathan, but instead of being able to get his brother back, he was as lost as ever. As lost as Billy seemed to be.

I moved closer. Billy was crying harder now—crying out his brother's name. Thick tears of frustration poured down his face. I grabbed him gently by his shoulders.

"Come away, Billy," I said quietly. "There is nothing you can do. You're just torturing yourself."

It took several goes before he started to pay attention to me. Then he turned and said, "I have to. He's my brother and I love him and he's trapped. He needs to be free from the Witch Tree. I have to do something."

He was beyond reasoning. Even if I dragged him away, his mind would stay locked to the tree unless I did something to free him, the way he wanted to free his brother.

I didn't want to get an adult to deal with this—that wouldn't help. I looked around for inspiration. Then I spotted something on the waste ground nearby.

"Come with me," I said. "I know what to do."

Billy didn't want to leave, but I started to drag him away from the tree. As I pulled him away, the grip on his mind seemed to ease and he started to walk by his own choice.

A few yards from the pavement, children had piled wood for a Guy Fawkes bonfire. Bits and pieces scavenged, begged, or stolen from the estate.

"Grab some of these and take them back to the tree," I said. "Pile them up around the base."

Billy grasped what I wanted to do and took an armful of wood back to the Witch Tree, dropping them at its foot. I had to pull him away again as he became hypnotized once more by the elaborate weaving pattern he saw, but the spell broke quicker this time. By the third load he turned away by himself.

Bit by bit we transferred all of the wood to the tree. I put my hand in my pocket and drew out my father's lighter. It was one of the few things I had to remind me of him.

I flicked it open and rolled the wheel against the flint, sparking the wick into life. The mist had made the wood slightly damp, but after thirty seconds or so a small twig caught fire. I blew on it gently, coaxing the flame until it danced across to some of the larger pieces of kindling. With a crackling whoosh, the fire started to grow and we stepped back from the growing heat.

Minute by minute more wood caught alight, and then the tree itself started to char and burst into flame. The dry bark caught first, flames rushing up the side of the Witch Tree towards the branches. Then the dead wood of the trunk smoldered and burnt, sending thick tendrils of black smoke into the air where it rolled in and out of Billy's ghost's dance. It filled me with joy. It felt good to do something for Billy.

He was staring up at the smoke and mist.

"The bigger the fire, the further away they can get," he said. "Some of them are flying away, like sparks from a Catherine Wheel."

The branches were bending in the heat and I could imagine they were flexing like fingers, trying to keep hold of the fleeing spirits.

Billy's face showed joy with each ghost he imagined escaping.

"He's broken away," Billy said. He looked up at the sky, then his eyes moved downwards as if tracking something swooping towards him. He raised his arms up and leaned his head back with an expression of joy on his face.

"He's free!" he shouted. Then he slumped and I grabbed him as he collapsed to the ground.

Of course, the police and fire brigade thought we were making it all up when they roared into the street with their sirens and lights waking up the residents. We were still too dazed to make up a suitable story and were taken down to the Police station where our families picked us up a few hours later.

Billy and I drifted apart after that, but I met his older brother once in town. He told me Billy was known affectionately as Little Napoleon. He had taken over Nathan's role in taking care of his siblings, despite being the youngest, and his love and support had meant his brother and sister had started to do well at school regardless of the indifference of their parents. It was as if he had taken on Nathan's spirit, his brother said. I just smiled.

Twelfth Pilgrim

Michael McCormick

Though I was a priest, mystery hadn't touched me over my long, dry years. I was an old man when it happened.

All in the Magdalen Order are expected to make a pilgrimage to the shrine of the holy relic of Mary the Younger at Stari Kirkevny, yet I stubbornly resisted this obligation for years.

"Too busy with parish affairs," I told my superiors.

So they assigned a junior priest to my parish. He was well-liked by all, including me. He quickly proved able at sermons, weddings, and funerals.

I lost my excuse. I had to go.

That summer I found myself in a remote province, hiking with eleven fellow pilgrims to the mountain shrine of Stari Kirkevny, each of us eager to kiss the ring of Mary Magdalene.

Some heretics say it's her betrothal ring, given by Jesus that last night at Gethsemane. Even if it's true, what's the harm? Judas betrayed Jesus hours later, so no marriage was consummated.

Twelve of us left Marienbad in our pilgrim robes, walking in silence, heads covered by hoods. Being old and slow, I trudged at the back of the group, lost in solemn thoughts of a cold draught at the village inn. Near me walked a tall woman of indeterminate age.

The woman stopped. The other pilgrims didn't notice. I passed by her, then looked back. I was going to inquire if she was alright, but she raised a slender finger to her lips, her face lost in shadow. She stepped abruptly into the woods.

Should I follow her? Should I call the other pilgrims? In the end, I did neither. I resumed walking behind the others. A buttery moon rose over distant mountains.

It was dark when we reached Stari Kirkevny. It looked more like a castle than a church. It seemed an odd place to keep Mary's ring. I was possessed by an absurd feeling that this was a false relic in a false church. Blasphemy, of course. The mountain altitude affected me.

The portal swung wide. A tall fellow, with a shaved head and glacier blue eyes, came out to greet us. As he looked us over, a queer expression contorted his face.

"You are eleven! Where is the twelfth?" he demanded in his guttural language.

The pilgrims murmured. They threw back their hoods and looked around, moonlight mixing with torchlight on their faces. No doubt it was a trick of the light, but they seemed to have the eyes of pigs. Their blue pig eyes fixed in my direction, as if the missing pilgrim was my fault.

I felt I was in danger. If I stayed with these pilgrims, entered their church, and kissed their false ring, I would never emerge again. At least not as the man I am now.

"You're a priest of the whore," the tall man barked in his rough tongue. "You know twelve is the required number. You bear the blame for this sacrilege."

Dread suffocated me. I fled to the woods. The pilgrims chased me with vengeful shouts. I left the path, plunging into dark underbrush, crashing into trees, wild boars grunting and squealing all around me, fireflies scattering, my boot catching a tree root. I plunged into peat and blackness.

It was still dark when I awoke. My pursuers were gone, but fireflies still flickered nearby.

Did I hear music?

A green light approached. To my amazement, a little man in a square hat emerged from the underbrush. He clutched a blade of grass on whose tip glowed a tiny lantern. He had mutton chop whiskers and brass spectacles.

A startled look crossed his face and he scampered away.

I knew I must be dreaming, but I stood up and looked for my miniature visitor. He was gone. I heard music again from the direction of the fireflies, so I headed that way, moving carefully in the dark.

A clearing pulsed with firelight and fiddles. A willow tree had fallen, leaving a broad stump. The trunk lay nearby, a nurse log sprouting toadstools and saplings.

A pilgrim's cloak was draped over the stump.

I recognized the twelfth pilgrim. She was dressed in white. She danced barefoot on the willow stump, face aglow from the fireflies.

Not fireflies! They had faces. On the ground, around the stump, tiny people laughed and danced and played fiddles. Waving his bobbing green lantern, I recognized the little man who surprised me before.

A twig snapped under my boot. The music stopped. The woman and little people turned to look at me.

Her face was kind but her eyes sternly penetrating.

"You're not like the others," she decided, her voice like crickets in summer.

"No," I admitted. "They chased me away."

She smiled.

"Join our dance!" she said.

Fiddle music began anew, fast and merry. I slipped off my boots and entered the clearing, careful to step over the wee folk.

The lady took my hands. We danced like children under the willow moon, twirling, and laughing, until exhaustion finally made me old again.

I woke under morning sunshine. She was gone, they were all gone.

I stood and stretched my bones, sore from running and dancing.

Something glittered on the stump. Though my aching back protested, I bent down for a closer look.

A gold ring. I picked it up. It bore markings like leaves and acorns.

I slipped it on my finger and never took it off again the rest of my living days. Over the years people asked me about it. To a trusted few I told the story of my pilgrimage. Among them was the young priest assigned to my parish.

Years passed. I retired and the younger fellow took over my duties. I lived out my days at my cottage, tending the garden, dreaming the dreams of old men.

One summer night I lay awake, looking out the garden window at a crescent moon, when I heard faint music. Someone was out there, near the willows, dressed in white.

I took off the ring and set it on my bedside table. I went out to the garden in my nightshirt. She took my hand in hers and smiled.

We walked into the woods, trailed by a procession of little folk. With each step, my bare feet sank deeper into the soil.

The ring that I left behind was placed on an altar in the parish church as an unofficial relic of Mary, known for its healing powers, though never sanctioned by the Church.

A young family lives in my cottage now. I like them. On moonlit nights, down by the old willow tree that I've become, the children sometimes hear merry music and join our dance.

Thoughts

Ginger Strivelli

Fred was eyeballing the box he'd pulled out of the meteorite. Well, he knew it wasn't a meteorite at all, now that he'd seen it up close. He thought it was, when he was streaking his riding lawn mower across the cow field trying to get to it as it landed. He still thought it was, as he climbed down into the impact crater to pull the silvery mass out. When he laid hands on it though, he instantly knew better. It was perfectly shaped and sized like a basketball—a little space ship. It was cool to the touch in spite of the fireball it had come down in, it was vibrating with some energy source, and it had a door. The door opened instantly and a small box slid out. Fred didn't know what to make of the tiny ship or the box. He decided to take them both back to his barn, before some shady government types showed up to take them away from him. He carried both objects back to the lawn mower and took off for the barn at top speed.

He stopped half way there, near the neighbor's fence where he knew their wifi sometimes worked. He took his cell phone out of his overalls' chest pocket and took pictures and video of both the ship and the box. Then he emailed them to himself and three trusted friends.

Just in case, he told them, someone took the find away from him.

He hurried on to the barn then snuck inside with his treasures. No one was following him yet, he noted, peeking out the barn door as he was barring it shut. He placed the ship and the box on his work bench table and sat down to inspect them closer.

Fred was a pig and cow farmer, not a scientist. It didn't take a scientist to figure out what the box was though. It was copper colored and rectangular. It had one large button with an open mouth on it. There was another smaller button with an inhuman, but recognizable, ear. It had a row of switches marked with dots. The first switch had one dot. The second switch had two dots. The third had three and so on through thirteen switches.

"It's a damn phone!" Fred said to no one, as he was alone in the barn except for the old, white donkey. Fred flipped the first switch and pushed the mouth button and said. "Hello?" tentatively. He then pressed the ear button and waited. He didn't have to wait long.

"Greetings unto you." A voice answered.

"What?" Fred stammered, but had forgotten to push the mouth button. He pushed it and repeated. "What?" Then he pushed the ear button again.

"Are you unable to comprehend my communication box's translation?" The voice asked.

"No, no, I understand it. Who... where are you?" Fred asked, working the right buttons.

"We are the Qeez people. We live on a planet three systems away from yours." The voice answered.

"How is it I can understand you and you can understand me?" Fred said, wondering if someone could be playing an elaborate hoax on him. "And how are we communicating instantly? These messages should be traveling back and forth between our planets—light years apart. There should be a delay. The transmissions can only travel as fast as light and you must be several if not hundreds of lightyears away. The delay should be years and years." Fred was no scientist, but he wasn't stupid.

"The communication box translates our thoughts. The transmission is instantaneous. There is no delay for light to travel between our planets. The technology does not depend on lightwaves."

"Yes, but nothing can travel faster than light." Fred reasoned.

"That is incorrect. Several kinds of matter, energy, and various spaceships travel faster than light. However, the communication box uses telepathic thought waves which travel instantaneously over any distance." The Qeez alien replied.

"Your spaceships travel faster than light?" Fred sat back and whistled.

"We do not have spaceships. The Qeez do not travel. We send forth our communication boxes to contact other races, but we stay put. There are other races who do travel and can travel faster than this light-speed limit you are so fixated on. The Marlo people could speak with you about their engine designs on their ships that travel nearly five times faster than that speed. Their switch number is seven. The Zeller people, switch three, also travel in ships that use engines rather than Stellar Transmission. All the others on the other switches use that form of travel."

"What the fresh hell is Stellar Transmission?" Fred said.

"I am not an engineer, but as I understand the process, a ship is flown into a star's magnetic field at a certain spot and angle, which transports the ship to the same spot in the field of another star. There are some like the Marlo and Zeller people who use simple speed instead due to their fragile bodies. My people do not travel either way as we stay put."

"Why do you not travel? Are your bodies even more fragile than the Marlo and Zeller?" Fred asked, leaning close to the box and wishing it had a button with an eye on it so he could see who he was talking to.

"No, we are not fragile at all. Our bodies are huge and strong, but we are stationary. We would starve if we traveled."

"You can't take food with you?"

"No."

"But you can take food when you travel about your planet, why not in space? Do you eat that much?"

"We eat and drink very much, yes. We eat and drink continuously. We do not travel about our planet. We stay put." The voice from the box explained.

Fred was confused. He was a farmer, a smart guy with a good education; he felt like he should be able to make more sense of the alien's words. "You never leave your city?"

"The translation box could not translate your last word. Please restate your question." The box spouted the reply.

"City... where you were born, where you live. Do you not explore other areas of your planet?"

"No. We never leave the spot of our birth. We live there till we die. Our remains stay put there, even after death."

Fred scoffed. "You don't even walk around?"

"The Marlo people walk. Other races fly, swim, crawl. We stand."

"Stand?" Fred said. "You just stand in the same spot forever?"

"Yes, our roots grow deep into the planet to get our water. Our limbs grow high into the air to get our food from the sunlight. We are drinking and eating constantly, as I explained before." The Qeez voice said patiently.

Fred whispered in disbelief. "You are a tree?"

"You do not have plants on your planet? I have never heard of a planet with only animals!" The voice whispered back, also in awe.

"No, no, we have plants." Fred said. "But they do not talk."

"I do not talk either, as I explained, you are hearing my telepathic thoughts translated by the communication box."

"But our plants do not have thoughts either." Fred said.

"Are you quite sure?" The alien asked.

"Well... no!" Fred whispered, sitting back to whistle again.

Mom's Tree

John Cady

I spent a handful of hours with my mom every weekend in her final years at the Shepard Home for the Elderly. She, however, spent most of those hours with the tree just outside her window. That is to say, her eyes would be fixated on it for much of my visit. She'd acknowledge me when I first got there. Sure. Once my pleasantries grew stale, however, it was like I wasn't there anymore.

The tree was there though—without fail. She could always count on it. I think it might have been her one constant. She never said so, but I think that's only because she couldn't find the words—or she didn't bother trying to find them. She just went right on staring at it like it was some beautiful painting in a museum.

She was all in a panic when I showed up with some lunch one Saturday.

"*They're taking it!*" she cried. "*They're taking it away from me!*"

She was so upset that her hands were shaking. I could tell she desperately wanted to do something about it. Only she couldn't. She was confined to her room—in her mind, she was anyways. In reality, I could have brought her right out there to raise a stink. But, what good would that have done? Whatever was going on outside that window honestly had nothing to do with her.

"Who is, Mom?" I asked.

She suddenly looked away from the goings-on out there to acknowledge me. By that point, her eyes were both sad and tired.

"The man," she replied, only slightly calmer now. "He's taking my tree."

I knew exactly who "the man" was. He was Mr. Morse, the groundskeeper. She wasn't a fan. I think she was too far gone by that point to realize he had a role there. She only saw him as an agitator—someone who disrupted the peacefulness of her day with all of his "little machines." Those little machines, as she put it, were his weed whacker, his lawn mower, and whatever else he needed to keep the grounds beautiful. He wasn't the friendliest guy in the world, but I suppose being a charmer wasn't one of the job requirements.

On this particular day, he used a chainsaw and a mini excavator. I was surprised the place would even spend the money on an excavator. Lord knows they went bargain basement on the interior of the building. Morse must have convinced them he needed one for the upkeep. Men and their toys.

"I'll go out and talk to him," I said, hoping it would calm her down some. "Maybe I can talk him out of it."

I knew the odds weren't in my favor. After all, he'd already begun digging. At least, she'd know I tried and that someone was on her side.

He was just finishing gassing up the chainsaw when I joined him out there. Thankfully, I wouldn't need to compete with it. He'd hear me loud and clear.

"Excuse me, sir?" I asked, breaking his concentration. He spilled some gasoline on his hands thanks to my interruption. I gasped. He was one of those people everyone seemed to walk on eggshells around—myself included, I guess.

"Yes?" he grumbled, clearly agitated. He wiped his hand up and down his thigh, leaving a grease smudge in the process. Those mustn't have been his good jeans.

"Sorry," I muttered.

Either he didn't accept it or he didn't hear it. The one thing I knew for sure was he didn't acknowledge it.

"What is it?" he asked. "I'm kind of busy here, in case you can't tell."

What a ray of sunshine he was. Some of the grumpy old men I'd encountered inside were more pleasant than him.

"Are you planning on taking this tree?" I asked. I knew before I asked. I just needed an opener.

"I am," he replied, matter-of-factly. "Why? You interested in it?"

Interested in it? As in to buy it?

"*Me?* No. Not really. I was just wondering what your plans were with it."

He looked at me as though I were on drugs. You'd have thought I asked him if he was going to finish his food scraps.

"It's just that if you don't have any specific plans for it, maybe you can just leave it there," I added. "It means a lot to my mother. She spends most of her day watching it. Honestly, it's all she looks forward to most days."

He shook his head in contempt. Imagine the nerve of someone making such a request.

"My plan is to get rid of it," he explained. "It's on its last legs. It's just taking up space now."

Jeez! How did he feel about some of the residents? Hopefully, he didn't say the same about them. It wouldn't have surprised me in the slightest.

"She'll be fine," he said, referring to Mom, not the tree. "Just aim her in a different direction."

What a lousy thing to suggest. Exactly how far gone did he think she was? I already wasn't what you'd consider a fan of his, but he'd definitely crossed the line with me now. I remained cool though. After all, a cooler head does prevail. I even chose to propose a business deal.

"Tell you what," I began. "I'll buy the tree. I'll write you a check right now. All I ask in return is that you leave it there until it dies."

He smirked.

"Or, until she dies," he replied, motioning to Mom's room.

My cooler head was heating up at an alarming rate. I hoped he'd accept my deal before I completely lost my shit. We were nearing that point for sure.

"So, do we have a deal?" I asked, so I wouldn't say what I really wanted to tell him.

He shook his head, and I could tell he was happy as a clam to deliver this final, crushing blow.

"We do not," he said. Having said this, he fired up his chainsaw, and gave me a wink. What a piece of work this guy was.

I turned and walked away just as he was bringing the blade to the tree. I didn't want to see him cut into it. It only would have angered me further. I could just make out his laughter as I opened the door to the lobby. He'd won. There was nothing I could do to stop him.

He nearly took down another tree on his way home that night. He evidently lost control of his Mustang, and wrapped it around a tree. It was over on Barrows Road. Never a good idea to fly down that stretch of road. It's lousy with curves.

Mom nearly burst into laughter when I told her about it the next afternoon. I pleaded with her not to celebrate it in front of any of his co-workers in case some of them actually liked him. It's unfortunate that he died, but I certainly wouldn't be losing any sleep over it. Nor would Mom, I imagined. Honestly, it's a shame it didn't happen a night earlier. She might have still had her tree.

"It's a shame that tree had to go before he did," she said nonchalantly.

"I know, Mom," I agreed. I figured there was no harm in saying it since there was no one else within earshot.

"Now, I've got nothing out there," she added. Woe was she. This man, even though he was a piece of garbage, had died a tragic death, and *she* was looking for sympathy.

"Say, maybe we can get my room moved," she suggested, with hope in her eyes.

Not likely. They had just lost one of their own. Moving her to a vacant room (should there have even been one available) probably wouldn't be happening for some time. I decided it was worth it to ask anyway. You never know.

Before I could get one word out, I happened upon one of the creepiest things at the nurses' station—or rather it was on the computer at the nurses' station. They were listening to a podcast about burial pods.

Evidently, corpses are good for trees. That is to say they help trees grow quicker and even fuller, according to some guest being interviewed. He claimed it had something to do with the nutrients that stick around in our bodies after we die.

"I wonder how they found that out," I said, interrupting the podcast. The nurse seated at the desk paused it, and turned to face me.

"Sorry," she apologized. "What was it you wanted, sir?"

I couldn't tell if she was being rude to me or if I'd completely caught her off guard. Whatever the case, I let the matter of burial pods rest and addressed my real reason for being there.

"Um, my mother is in room eighteen," I began.

She glanced beyond me to Mom's room, and then nodded.

"She was wondering if she could, perhaps, switch rooms."

Without even checking for herself, she directed me to the whiteboard on the wall behind her. Written upon it was every resident's name (including Mom's) along with their room number.

"Sorry," she apologized, once again. "Every room is taken."

Just what I didn't want to hear. More bad news for Mom. I turned and trudged on back to her room. I found her staring at the vacant spot where her tree once stood.

"Sorry, Mom. No luck. Every room is taken."

She sulked. She was devastated. Years earlier, prior to living there, I would have told her it was just a tree. Nothing could be taken for granted anymore though. In this chapter of her life, a favorite tree held a lot more weight. Even though it was out of my hands in both instances, I felt like I'd failed her.

My guilt soon gave way to anger however. I wasn't angry with the nurse. There really wasn't anything she could do either. The one I was angry with was already dead and soon to be buried.

I thought about him rotting for all eternity in some cemetery somewhere. It briefly brought a smile to my face. I figured at least some good would come of this, but then, I thought about Mom and her tree, once again. All that remained of it was the hole he left behind with his goddamn excavator. I wished to hell I could have crammed him down into that hole.

It was then that a thought crossed my mind. It was a morbid one for sure, but I'd be lying if I said it didn't bring a smile back to my face. Morse was going in that hole, and a tree was going right on top of him: Mom's tree. I mean, I didn't have one of those burial pods or even the slightest idea where I might find one, but I figured I'd take my chances with stuffing him down in there anyways.

Before any of this could become a reality, though, I first needed to get to him before he got to his casket. Once he was in there, I'd be shit out of luck.

It wasn't difficult to find out who was burying him. All I needed to do was keep an eye on the local obituaries.

The Henderson Funeral Home looked like it hadn't seen a renovation of any kind in decades. Had they been taking one of my loved ones, then I might have had something to say about it—if only to my fellow family members. For what I had in mind, though, I was thrilled that they hadn't updated the place. Everything looked dated, and I was sure the security system was no exception.

I decided the best way to get a good look at the place—the outside of it anyways—was to bring my dog, Baxter, for a walk in their neighborhood. People tend to pay you no mind when you're out walking your dog, even if they've never seen you in their part of town.

There was a garage down back, which I initially found odd, but I guess it made sense. You have to park the hearse somewhere. It was a pretty basic setup, no security code or anything. To be fair, though, I doubt many car thieves out there were jonesing for a hearse. They're probably difficult to hide, and I doubt there are many buyers. There was a regular door adjacent to the garage door. It would be my point of entry and our point of exit—mine and Morse's.

A couple of nights prior to his wake, I went ahead and sprung him. Believe it or not, all I needed to get inside was a credit card of mine that had expired four months earlier. I slid it right down between the door and its frame, moved it around rapidly once I reached the lock, and, within seconds, I heard it unlock. I turned the knob, and entered.

It didn't take long to find him. He and another guy were behind door number two. Door number one opened to a stairway leading to, I assume, the main floor.

The other guy was pretty old. If I had to guess, I'd say he died of natural causes. Morse was already in his burial suit thankfully. The old guy, meanwhile, was in his birthday suit. He might have just arrived that afternoon.

I'd left my car parked right outside the door, with the trunk wide open. I had entertained the idea of just shoving him in the backseat, but that could have gone wrong any number of ways. He could have stunk to high heaven. I could have been pulled over for my broken taillight, which had been that way for quite some time. You'd have thought I would have had the good sense to have it fixed that week since I was planning on stealing a corpse.

I covered him up with an old blanket I had in there. It was a beach blanket, so it was plenty big enough. I also had the tree I'd picked up at a nursery earlier in the day in there, along with a shovel and a knife. The shovel was for digging his new grave, and the knife was for poking him up.

Once I arrived at my destination, the Shepard Home for the Elderly, I retrieved the shovel and snuck around back to where Mom's room was. Luckily, their security system was every bit as effective as the one at the funeral home.

I drove the blade of my shovel into the ground where Mom's tree had been. It was still soft and broken up, so it would take no time at all to make any headway. I dug down pretty far and out just as far in every conceivable direction. I had to. I needed it large enough to hold the former groundskeeper. I nearly burst into laughter when it dawned on me that the poor sap had unknowingly helped me dig his own grave.

Nearly ten minutes had passed before I was satisfied. I couldn't take any chances. I really couldn't have him anywhere near the surface.

Back at the car, I popped the trunk, and grabbed hold of my knife. I then repeatedly drove it into his torso. I stuck him just about everywhere you could think of; and, just so you know, there was a method to my madness. I surmised that the more punctures in him, the better; it would leave his remaining nutrients with more ways to escape. I'm not going to lie though; for a time, I was thinking about what he said about Mom as I stabbed away at him.

When I was finished, I hoisted him over my shoulder and carried him around back to his freshly dug grave. Once there, I wasted no time at all in dropping him right down into it. He didn't land quite how I had envisioned it. His ass was in the air, with his head turned to the side in the dirt. What a way to spend eternity, I thought. I chuckled beneath my breath, and then proceeded to fill the hole in.

The picture was nearly complete. All that was missing was the piece de resistance —the tree. Correction: Mom's new tree.

It took me no time at all to retrieve it from the car. I carefully positioned it in the ground—a good foot or so above Morse's ass—and shoveled the rest of the dirt into its base. I then stamped the dirt down flat, and made sure the tree was as sturdy as could be. Barring a gust of hurricane force wind, that tree should remain there for as long as the next groundskeeper sees fit.

Fun fact: Yours truly applied for the job the very next morning. They claimed I was overqualified, and that I'd probably be making less than I was at my other job. But I told them I felt a real connection to the place.

That morning, Mom was all too happy to show me the new tree someone had planted for her right outside her window.

"It's like they planted it just for me," she said, beaming.

I happily nodded.

The Magical Forest

Shari Held

As a child, Adrienne had believed magic lived in their forest. Sometimes she'd glimpsed fairies lounging on toadstools or elves sleeping on hammocks high in the sugar maple trees. She was sure of it. But when she'd stopped to take a closer look, nothing was there. Nothing except the feeling that she wasn't the only living being in the forest.

Now thirty, she'd inherited her parents' small farm and the adjoining forest. She was at one of those fork-in-the-road, life-changing situations. Keep the farm or sell it? She rubbed her temples and stepped to the porch for some fresh air.

As if it knew what she needed, the forest beckoned to her. She found herself walking down that familiar path to the heart of the forest. Once there, she caressed the trunk of the majestic old spruce she'd named the Wishing Tree as the breeze softly whispered through its branches. When she was younger, she'd thought birthday wishes made on the tree would come true. She closed her eyes and surrendered to the comfort these memories gave her. It was the first peace she'd enjoyed since receiving word of her parents' car accident.

The next day, Adrienne began toying with the idea of keeping the farm—giving up her corporate marketing job and moving back home full-time. It wouldn't be a big sacrifice. Secretly, she was bored with her job. Tired of the whole corporate attitude. She'd miss her Starbucks, but hey, you could order anything online these days.

Plus, a friend of her parents had told her she could make the farm self-supporting by leasing out the farmland. Of course, she'd have to sell the forest timber to pay for clearing the land.

And there was her dilemma. Could she literally kill the forest and the Wishing Tree, her old childhood friend?

She called Dani, her other childhood friend, who still lived in town. Dani had been her main support since she'd arrived home nearly two weeks ago. She'd run it by her.

"Hi, Dani. Do you have a few minutes?"

"Sure. What's up?"

"I'm seriously thinking about staying here—trying to make a go of the farm."

"That's fantastic! I'll bring a bottle of champagne. Cook's will have to do—no Dom Perignon in this little town."

"Hold on. It's not that easy."

"Why? What's stopping you?"

"To make a living, I'll have to rent out the land to farmers. And making the land rentable will require a lot of capital. I'll have to level the forest and sell the timber." Her voice trembled.

"Aw, sweetie. I know how much you love the forest. So do I. It was our favorite playground when we were growing up. But you're not ten anymore. You have to be practical."

Hearing Dani say it didn't make it any easier, but it reinforced what Adrienne knew deep in her gut. "You're right," she said, sighing. "It's time to see things through adult eyes. Time to let the forest go. I don't see any other option. Dad had things set up but hadn't yet signed the paperwork before... um, before... the accident. Mom talked him out of it several times before, but it looks as if he was going through with it this time." Adrienne took in a deep breath and stiffened her jaw. "I'll call the company today and tell them it's a go."

* * *

A tear slid down Adrienne's cheek as she watched the working crew set up for the job. She pulled the curtains and inserted her earbuds to protect her from the gut-wrenching sight and bone-chilling sound of the chainsaws.

Abruptly, all sound ceased. Adrienne removed her earbuds. An eerie quiet greeted her, soon broken by someone banging on her door.

"Sorry to bother you, ma'am," the foreman said, "but our machinery broke down." He scratched his nearly bald head. "I figure it's some kind of electronic malfunction. We'll be back as soon as we get it fixed."

Adrienne just nodded at him. She couldn't decide whether the reprieve made her feel relieved or if it only prolonged her sadness.

That night, she felt the urge to enjoy one last walk in the forest. She longed to capture the look and feel of the magical forest deep down in her bones. If it had to go, it would live forever in her memory.

When she arrived in the center of the forest, she ran her hand down the trunk of the Wishing Tree. "Goodbye, my old friend," she whispered.

"Ouch!" Her finger bled from a tiny sliver of embedded bark. She'd have to remove it with tweezers so her finger didn't get infected. As she turned to head back home, a bumblebee buzzed around her head.

That's not possible, it's nighttime. Bees aren't active once the sun goes down.

Adrienne changed her tune as it stung her, not once, but twice. She picked up her pace and produced a big sigh of relief when she finally reached her front door. It was quickly replaced with a cry of dismay.

The outdoor lighting revealed her Lexus, which she'd parked in the shade of an old tree, was scratched. Could wind-tossed branches have swiped the car? She didn't recall it being that windy. But then she'd never seen bees fly at night, either. She shivered and rubbed her arm where the bee had stung her.

More surprises awaited her at the front of the house. Raccoons had torn up the porch planters and knocked them to the ground; a trail of scat littered the porch. The flowerbeds she'd tended since she arrived looked like the Indianapolis Colts had used them for practice.

Once inside, Adrienne did something she'd never done before. She locked the front door.

Late that night she was awakened by screeching, squealing, and the rustling of tree branches. She jumped out of bed, draped a shawl over her white gown, grabbed a flashlight, and headed for the forest. Maybe her mind was playing tricks on her, but it seemed as though the trees had moved closer to one another, creating a kind of barricade.

I must be crazy to even think that. It's just my imagination, spurred on by guilt. That's all.

But Adrienne wasn't taking any chances. She hightailed it back to the house and called Dani, who promised to spend a couple days at the farm with her, starting first thing tomorrow.

* * *

The workmen arrived early the next day with the repaired machinery. But no sooner had they started working than it broke again, this time injuring one of the workers.

"I'm telling my crew to call it a day," the foreman told Adrienne and Dani. "The guys are kind of spooked. I'm going in there to see what I can find."

The foreman never returned.

His truck was still parked in the driveway at four o'clock. Adrienne and Dani searched for him, but gave up at dusk, figuring the other men found him on the far side of the property and gave him a ride.

In the deep of the night, the strange noises started in again: screeching, squealing, rustling, and screaming.

"What's that?" Dani asked, clutching her robe around her. "It's coming from the forest."

"I don't know, but I'm going to find out," Adrienne said, running down the stairs and grabbing a knife from the kitchen. "You stay here."

"No way I'm letting you go by yourself," Dani said, snatching a lantern from the countertop. "Here, we'll need this."

Both women hastened down the path, Adrienne in the lead. They saw nothing amiss, and the sounds broke off when they entered the forest.

Adrienne stopped abruptly and Dani slammed into her. "Oh my god! Dani, don't look. You won't want to see this."

The lantern's glow revealed the foreman's body. It was wedged between two trees that appeared to have crushed him. But that wasn't possible. At least not in an *ordinary* forest.

With a piercing flash of awareness Adrienne recalled her ninth birthday. That was the year her father had first considered clearing the forest. She'd cried and pleaded, but he couldn't be moved. In her anger, she'd run to the Wishing Tree and wished that anyone who tried to harm the forest would die a horrible death. Fortunately, her father decided to leave the forest intact.

But Adrienne had a sickening suspicion the forest hadn't forgotten about that wish. She shoved the lantern into Dani's hand "Run, Dani, run!" she cried. "And don't look back."

Both women began running, but it was difficult to see in the pitch dark. Tree branches whipped menacingly in the fierce wind, their tendrils wrapping abound the girls' throats. Tree roots bubbled up out of the ground and tripped them, impeding their retreat.

Then the howling began.

Dani whimpered.

Adrienne brandished her knife against the tree branches, but soon realized she was fighting a losing battle. She surrendered and threw down her knife. The howling stopped. The trees moved closer, hemming both women in, drawing them nearer to the Wishing Tree.

Nothing was visible except vague shapes. But the shuffling noise as the trees moved ever closer to the heart of the forest and the rustling of their tree branches in the stark silence was terrifying. Inch-by-inch, the trees crept closer to the women and began to cover them. Adrienne felt as if the life was being squeezed out of her. Dani was no longer struggling, but Adrienne knew she was alive because she could hear her raspy breath.

Adrienne began to cry. "Please let her go," she begged the Wishing Tree. "She has nothing to do with this. It was me. I made a mistake when I made that wish. Please don't hurt her. And if you let me live, I promise I'll have it declared a wildlife refuge. No harm will come to the forest. It will stay just as it is forever."

Strange guttural, non-human sounds came from the Wishing Tree. Seconds later, the limbs of the trees enclosing her and Dani loosened and withdrew. The women were bruised and battered, but saved. Just like the forest.

* * *

The next morning Adrienne had two calls to make. One to the police about the foreman's body and one to call off the deforestation job. The coroner ruled the foreman's death an accident—figured he'd run into a tree and knocked a limb down on himself in the process. Adrienne and Dani answered a few questions, and the police team wrapped up its business fairly quickly.

Although it was closer to noon than six o'clock, Adrienne made blueberry pancakes while Dani brewed Starbucks French Roast coffee and squeezed fresh orange juice. They decided to eat on the patio, overlooking the forest.

"What did the company say when you told them you'd decided not to go through with the deforestation?"

"Actually, the salesperson sounded relieved. After what happened with the foreman and the injuries one of the other workers sustained, it was having trouble finding anyone who wanted to come back."

Dani stirred creamer in her coffee. "What do you think really happened out there?" She looked down at her arms, which bore no marks to indicate she'd been attacked by living trees.

Adrienne shivered. "I don't know. But I think it's better if we don't try too hard to figure it out. Or mention it to anyone else."

"Sounds good to me," Dani said, taking a quick sip of hot coffee. "I doubt you'll be able to get me to go on a picnic in the forest any time soon." She smiled. "Just sayin'." She got up, gathered her things, and hugged Adrienne. "You be careful."

"I will. But I think everything will be just fine now."

After Dani left, Adrienne poured another cup of coffee and studied her forest. Almost without being aware of it, she found herself walking down the path to her old friend the Wishing Tree. She closed her eyes and rested her head on its trunk. She felt at peace once more. A rustling noise caught her attention. She raised her head and saw an elf scurrying along the forest floor. She was sure of it.

The Swamp that Ran Scarlet

Willow Croft

Susie smelled something burning. She ran down the porch steps and yanked her dinner off the cooking fire.

Can't afford to be careless, but all she could think of was the cleared swath of swampland she'd discovered earlier that day. She ladled her dinner onto a plate just as a scarlet ibis blazed its way past the dun-colored cypress trees. Susie sat back down into her old rocking chair and listened to the hidden insects talk to each other. She wished she could answer them right back.

But she hadn't inherited that gift.

"Sometimes it skips a generation," her momma always used to say, followed up by, "now, when are you gonna have kids?"

But the swamp was her child. Her child, and now her only family, since Momma had died the year before. She finished her dinner just as a barred owl began to hoot from the live oak right near the stilt house. Susie scraped her plate over the porch railing and rinsed it in the water bucket. Once inside, she pulled her favorite book off the shelf and started to read about the little girl and her secret garden. Unlike the girl in the story, she couldn't protect her swamp from development. She closed the book with a snap and shoved it onto the nightstand, nearly knocking the lantern off. In her sleep, she saw the swamp as it had been when she was a child. When it spread out as far as her eye could see, farther than she could run, even.

"*It's your secret*," the owl hooted to her in her dream. And she was the oak tree and the owl, all at once, until she took flight on the owl's wings, gliding over the tangled growth of the swamp. The moon rose before her in the sky, blazing a strange scarlet against the dark night. A swoop, and she was diving downwards, towards the shimmering waterways of the swamp. The scarlet-tinged water moved slowly, sinuously past the knobbly cypress trees and through the arched roots of the mangroves. It looked like blood. The blood of a dying swamp, she thought, and the water reached up to caress her wings with its rising mist.

"Save us," the red mist whispered.

"But how?" she whispered back.

And it told her, just before the mist faded back into the earth. It wasn't all gone, though.

In its place was a thorny, twisted plant with flowers as red as the moon that glowed above her.

* * *

The sun beating in through the window woke her. Outside, it was even brighter. She rubbed her eyes as she made her way to the spring. She'd just reached the edge of the grasses that lined the stream when she saw it. She blinked, and rubbed her eyes again. It was still there, sprouting up on the bank, just as it had been in her dream.

She set the bucket down and crept up on the plant with the red flowers.

Like it could get up and run away, she thought. She remembered what the red mist had told her, and she gently removed a handful of leaves from the plant.

Boil water, and steep the leaves. She dunked the bucket into the stream and hurried back.

The leaves gave off a pungent smell, and she added tea and sugar to the water bubbling over the now-crackling fire. When the tincture darkened, she poured it into her canteen.

Cool it in the stream. She didn't remember the red mist telling her that, but maybe she was finally able to understand the language of the swamp, just as all the women in her family before her had.

The sun was reaching the midday mark, and she lifted the canteen from the mangrove-shaded stream. She didn't need the memory of the dream to tell her where to go; she already knew.

The mist had also shown her the man. But the sight of him, standing at one edge of the cleared swampland, made her angry all the same. Even worse was the row of stakes spread out behind him. The bright red plastic ribbons that topped the stakes fluttered in the breeze.

He's marking the site for construction. And she knew it was the first of many more new homes to come. Don't let your anger show.

"Hiya there," she called out.

The man nearly dropped the rest of his wooden stakes as he spun around. "What the . . ."

"Hiya there," she said again. "Whatcha doing?"

"Young lady, you sure startled me." He looked her up and down. "Sweetie, are you lost?"

Creep. "No, sir. Just out for a hike," she said.

"Here?" He stopped eyeballing her long enough to look around him. "Why would anyone want to hike through this muddy pit?" He slapped at a mosquito on his arm.

Susie tried not to glare at him. "I reckon there's no other spot like it. It's real pretty back in here. If you know what to look at."

"Miss, the only thing worth looking at out here will be the brand-new housing development we're gonna build. Just wait till you see the landscape we're putting in—hired a designer from up north. It's gonna be beautiful—a real work of art." He pulled a tissue out of his pocket and wiped his face with it. It left little white pieces all over his face.

"You look mighty hot. Got some cool iced tea here." She held up her canteen. "You want some?"

"Well, that's very kind of you. I left my water bottle back in my car. I've never been this hot before." He stared at her canteen with the same fixation as he'd stared at her, just before.

That's what happens when you cut down all the trees. For a moment she saw red that had nothing to do with mists or moonlight or scarlet ibises. She took a deep breath and held out her canteen. The man unscrewed the top and wiped off the canteen's mouth with the remnants of his tissue. He took a long drink and handed it back to her.

"Thank you, miss. That just hit the spot," he said.

She watched as he bent over to jab another red-ribboned stake into the ground. The plant's effects took hold faster than she expected, and the man's hand began to shake. The stake fell to the ground.

"What the . . ." The man tried to straighten up, but he swayed and fell with a thump next to the stake he'd dropped.

She flipped him over. His eyes stared up at the sky, unblinking. She took hold of his arm and pulled him back into the trees. She waded deeper into the swamp until the man's body bobbed up and down next to her. She pushed him further out into the slow-moving current, and then splashed the water noisily.

"Gators'll take care of you, soon enough, don't you worry," she told the floating body.

She collected every last stake from the clearing and tossed them into the rekindled fire back at the house. The plastic ribbons gave off a sickening odor as they burned, and she had to scrape bits of melted red plastic out of the fire's ashes once it died down.

"Beautiful, my ass," she said, laughing. A scrub-jay squawked a complaint and flew off.

She stared at the few remaining glowing coals, and the sky behind it turned a darker shade of blue.

It was done. Done just as the mist told her to do.

The moon rose, a regular pale white glow, and she waited. Far off in the distance, she heard the owl call. This time, she didn't follow it. She knew it wasn't for her. It was part of the night's magic, and she'd lived in the swamp long enough to know when to let things be. She didn't even dare to sleep, to risk her dream-self interfering.

* * *

Just as soon as the sun began to turn the sky pink, she started off into the swamp. She had to see if it worked. She dodged cypress knees, but the swamp didn't seem to be getting any shallower. Or any drier. She had to be in the clearing. Or what was the clearing.

She'd done it.

It had worked.

The swamp was back. She felt tears well up in her eyes. She circled around the former clearing, touching every tree to make sure they were real. She was on the far side when she heard voices. She ducked further back into the restored thicket of mangrove trees.

* * *

"I don't understand. GPS says that this is the right place. And Charles reported that this had already been drained, and filled in. In fact, he was coming out here to get an early start on the site survey." A man in a suit pushed his way through a clump of mangroves on the opposite side.

Susie tried not to giggle as he squelched through the mud. She heard him curse.

Another man joined him. He was dressed in jeans and sneakers, and didn't seem to mind the wet swamp. He laughed as the man in the suit nearly fell into a mangrove tree.

"Don't laugh, Anthony. These shoes are Italian leather." She watched as he held onto a mangrove branch and tried to shake his shoes dry.

"I told you not to wear them out here, Jack. Besides, since when has Charles been reliable? Or, perhaps, even sober?" The man named Anthony frowned as he looked around.

"You're right. He's probably still asleep in his room back at the hotel. Why didn't we think to check before we left?" The man called Jack shifted his attention to his other shoe.

"These are ruined. I'm going to kill Charles when we get back."

Too late, Susie thought.

She saw Anthony scan the area. She drew back deeper into the mangrove thicket. She couldn't see the men anymore, but that meant they couldn't see her.

"You know, it really is pretty out here," she heard Anthony say. "Almost like a garden."

"Are you kidding? It's disgusting. I've half a mind to give up on the whole project. Who would want to live out here, anyway?" Jack asked.

"Well, we've invested a lot of capital. And I'm not going to lose my investment. We're continuing the project," Anthony said. "I'll arrange for a crew to come out to clear and drain area. I'll oversee it myself; make sure it gets done."

Susie heard the two men slosh back the way they came. She frowned. She knew what she had to do. What she had to keep doing, to protect the swamp. To protect her garden. She was the wall that would keep this all secret. And she would be a strong one.

Tête de Bois

Liam Hogan

"What will it be, sir?"

George Monkton slumped on a barstool at the oak-wood bar, running his hands slowly over the cool surface. Conversation as soothing as music trickled from the shadowy booths around him. For now, George had the barman's attention all to himself.

He couldn't remember how or indeed *where* he'd found this bar, but that wasn't so unusual. Nor that he'd lost the colleagues he'd been drinking with when the pubs had closed, the beer sitting heavy in his stomach. But he wasn't done, he just needed to change tack. Less volume, more alcohol. He'd have a hangover in the morning, sure. That dull, wooden feeling the French call *une tête de bois*. A head of wood. But that wouldn't be any worse than the tedium of another day's management consulting.

This wasn't the first time George had peeled away to find cocktails. Somehow, perhaps through sheer dogged persistence, he always managed to sniff them out. He *lived* for these unreal, liminal hours set adrift betwixt one day and the next, times when a glance at his watch told him nothing useful at all.

The black-shirted barman, his top button casually undone, stood arms akimbo before serried ranks of backlit bottles. His almost feminine fingers splayed across the burnished wood of the long bar. An elevated shelf with single malts of implausible vintages winked in duplicate from the age-specked mirror. George caught a glimpse of a disheveled man sitting at the bar, and for a hazy instant, as he stared into his unfamiliar reflection, the barman's slicked-back hair became long and unruly, the nose pierced by a thin shard: either horn, or bone, or perhaps flint. The hawkish face was daubed blue with strange glyphs. A *shaman.*

George shook his fuzzy head, and there the barman was again, front and centre, neatly groomed and patiently waiting. Very well. He'd been about to order his usual, but would instead leave it in the lap of the gods.

"What do you suggest?" he replied, voice midnight hoarse.

The barman quirked a sleek eyebrow. "Well sir, you have the look of a man who likes an old fashioned—"

George sat straighter, a leer playing across his doughy face.

"—but, if I may be so blunt with a customer I have not had the pleasure of serving before, I think you order one as a test of a barman's patience as much as his competence, and don't really enjoy them as you once did."

George frowned. Was that true?

"For this reason," the bartender blithely continued, "I recommend choosing something *new.* Something to lighten your jaded mood." He turned on legs that seemed to bend the wrong way, though that was patently impossible, bringing back a trio of bottles.

"Absinthe?" George croaked, eyeing the glowing green liquor trapped behind shining curves.

"You *might* know it as such," conceded the barman. "*This* is the drink that inspired today's pale and timid imitations. This is wormwood, the spirit of rebellion, of art. The soul of Paris. This is *la fée verte*—the original green fairy."

The barman tapped a manicured nail against the crystal, and a mournful chime mocked the room's gentle hubbub. Something stirred in the deep emerald depths, and George had the uneasy feeling he was being watched.

"I don't much like aniseed," he sniffed and turned to the middle bottle, a slender teardrop of paper-thin porcelain, the glaze a web of tiny cracks and, at its impossible summit, a chunky wax-sealed stopper on a thick red cord. "What's this?"

"Ah! A most mischievous spirit from the East. It hails from the cradle of civilization and has been responsible for as many downfalls as rises. Smoke and incense; the dry heat of a desert. Everything you could possibly wish for."

"Hmm," George murmured, turning to the most curious of the three containers. It appeared to have been carved from a single gnarled hunk of wood, the bark a stubborn blackness with a deep hint of red. The "bottle" branched into a lopsided Y, one limb petering out into a rough, thorny stub, the other planed smooth and stoppered with a splintered wedge. George wondered how much liquid such an inefficient receptacle could possibly hold and where they stuck the barcode?

"Closer to home, this one," the barman said, voice reverently low. "The spirit of *ancient* woods. From when these isles were thick with dark forests, places of mystery and power that predate the Norman invasion, predate Christianity, predate even the Romans and *their* pantheon of gods."

"Yes," George said, shaking his befuddled head. "But what *is* it?"

"A heady blend of botanicals and the rarest of nectars. The base distilled from the most venerable of yew trees."

George squinted, suspicious. "Isn't yew poisonous?"

"As is wormwood, as indeed is alcohol. It's all in the careful preparation and distillation and—"

"OK, OK," muttered George, battling the sudden fear he was sobering up. "You don't need to blind me with the *science*. How do you take it?"

"Very, very carefully," the barman grinned. "Straight up for preference, or with the merest splash of spring water. This is not a drink for the faint of heart. This is for men hewn from oak." He unstoppered the wooden flask. A faint mist, redolent of moss and autumn leaves, rolled from the stout neck, wafting George's way. The fumes were intoxicating.

"I'll take a shot of the wood," he nodded, brusquely, eagerly.

"As you *wish*, sir."

* * *

The soft patter of conversation resonated around and through him. He was in a dimly lit bar, but it took a long moment to work out it was the same one as before. There was something distinctly unsettling about his current perspective.

A man approached, an unsteady lurch to his gait. Half, perhaps three-quarters cut. His suit rumpled, watery eyes blinking behind smeared glasses. A fellow denizen of the night. The stranger grabbed onto George for support.

George tried to shrug him off, but found he could not. He couldn't *move* at all. For a moment he panicked, until he sensed the companionship of others, so many others: men lost to a night that stretched back to the dawn of time. A night that would, for George and all of these welcoming souls, never end.

The stranger's hands ran questioningly over his smooth, cool wooden flank. George shivered in response.

Two more hands, long and thin, almost feminine, pressed reassuringly down, deadening the tremor before the stranger could feel it.

"What will it be, sir?" the barman asked with an inviting smile.

The Birchies

James Ryan

"So why are you telling me what you did?" he asked, the snarl twitching his lips slightly.

"Look, I have to tell someone, Colonel," the other man replied, his glasses helping to make his eyes look wider than the panic evident in his voice.

"Okay, so tell me again. You're Doctor Pine, from—"

"No, I'm not a doctor. I only just graduated high school."

"Okay... Norman, right? High school student Norman Pine, who somehow is this genetic whiz. So far, what I got is right?"

"No, Colonel, I'm not a gene whiz. I had access to my friend Laurel's portable CRISPR setup. Her older brother had one in the garage, and when he went to California for two weeks, we played around with it." Exasperated, he added, "CRISPR: It's a do-it-yourself gene editing tool; he brought it home between semesters, so he could work on it to complete his graduate degree project."

"This tool... the older brother just left it there, lying around?"

"She hacked the locks and downloaded some operating instructions."

“So, you two played around with this... gene editing machine, huh?”

“We honestly didn’t know what would happen.”

“So, what did you kids do?”

“We tried to—” Norman got very quiet.

“If anything helpful’s going to be accomplished by you, you need to be straight with me. And if it’s what I think it is, then what you did with the CRISPR is probably a lot worse than what you’re trying to hide.” The Colonel leaned in and said in a conspiratorial half-whisper, “You wanted to make drugs, right?”

“Yes . . .?”

“See, now you’re being helpful. So, that’s how we got the Birchies, right?”

“You knew?”

“We knew, from the samples of the Birchies we got, that someone tried to splice cannabis and psilocybin mushroom genes. A theory suggested that it was someone looking for a new high. This just confirms that.”

“And you’re not upset?”

“Really? Are you really asking me if I’m upset that you two screw-ups played with this, tried to fuse that with a birch tree, and created the worst invasive plant since kudzu?”

Norman started to visibly twitch as the Colonel glowered.

“Oh, trust me, you can bet that whatever punishment you two f-ups get from a tribunal for creating the Birchies, there won’t be enough of your asses left for me to do anything more to you.”

Norman tried to look at the Colonel without flinching as the berating went on. “You mean what’s going to happen to me, you mean?”

“Oh, let me guess: You came forward to give yourself up, and you want us to be lenient on your girlfriend, right? What makes you think she’s not going to be in trouble with us the same as you?”

“She was at Paramus.”

The Colonel’s threatening demeanor shut off right away. “Oh, I’m sorry. I didn’t know she was there.”

“It was horrible. I watched it on a FaceTime call with her. I watched her when she... I, I didn't know that they weaponized pollen like that."

"No one did, son. That was the first time we saw the pollen clouds. You don't have to tell me more about what happened if—"

"It was the Type II."

"Crap," the Colonel tried to whisper.

"I watched her go through a pollen cloud as she was trying to hide. I watched the tendrils sprout all over her... it was quick, the way she got turned to mulch right in front of me."

"She and a few hundred other people at that massacre. That was just a warm up for what they did to New York."

Norman started to fall apart, his posture collapsing as his spine unknitted out of alignment.

"It's horrible what the Birchies have done," the Colonel continued. "We lost New England and the east coast to them in only three weeks, hundreds of thousands dead at the feet—well, roots—of a tree that grows like a weed on speed once it gets protein. Which wouldn't be that bad if they didn't keep adapting new ways to catch and trap any animals they can, like us. I hope you can live with the knowledge of what you've done."

"But that's why I'm here. Anything I can do to make this right. I have the files, the notes of what we did when we used the CRISPR setup. The original genes for what became the Birchies, that's got to be of some value, right?"

"The way these keep evolving every time a batch of them get to dine on someone, or someone's pets? I don't know if that'd help that much. I can run it up to the R&D trust and see what kind of intel..."

Norman turned to look at the Colonel as the silence grew, watching as the Colonel's brows merged into one...

"I'm going to ask a delicate question. Your call with Laurel: Is there any chance you snapped some images of what was happening to her when you two were talking?"

Norman just stared at the Colonel with eyes wider than a tree's crown.

"That may be out of line, son," the Colonel said. "I don't mean to ask something like that, but the R&D folk are looking for any intel on the Type II pollen. It was a long shot, and I'm just asking for something like that. I'd understand you're upset."

Norman shook a little before replying, "I recorded the call."

The Colonel looked at him.

"It was an accident; I was distracted because she called suddenly while I was doing something else, and my thumb accidentally hit the record button on the phone. I, I found the file before I came here; I, I didn't know you'd need that."

"Norman, if the R&D folk can get any clues from that call as to how the Type II pollen works, that could help us get troops out there with saws and flamethrowers to close distance and take the fight straight to them. Laurel won't have died in vain if this allows us to turn the tide."

"So . . . I actually did something good, here?"

"I am still going to bust your ass into a million pieces for releasing blood-drinking fast-rooting trees on humanity. But, if this saves us all, maybe not into that many pieces . . ."

Where They Fear to Tread

Ray Daley

Had it truly been only five hours since they'd caught me? My legs were telling me it felt like a lot longer, my feet were too. My right arm was starting to lose feeling now as well.

I guess it didn't help much that they were constantly pushing me to keep moving. Again, I got the cold, stony hand in my back.

"Man, move! We must be out before daylight!"

I blew out a hard gasp of air. "Listen! I need to rest longer than a few moments. Humans simply aren't equipped to keep moving for a long time." That was a lie, people had amazing endurance. I knew of ultra-runners, men who had survived the Japanese death marches. I just hoped they didn't know any of those things.

The big one grabbed something out of the darkness, just plucking the object out of the inky black of deep night. It had heard the movement nearby, just like I had. The beast towered over me; it was at least twenty feet tall. It brandished the catch in front of me. "You, man! Safe to eat?"

I had to wait a few seconds for my night vision to improve, so I could make out what the thing had caught.

Oh. It was a deer, or at least it had been, before the beast had crushed the poor thing in its grip. "For me, when cooked, yes. For you? No."

It just grunted its displeasure at me. "Must find food soon. Or... "

Yeah. It didn't need to expand any further on that threat. All of the creatures had made that threat at least once since I had been captured. I guess I should start by explaining how I got in this mess in the first place.

* * *

I had been hiking in the woods. Sure, I knew it was forbidden, but I knew the area like the back of my hand, having grown up here. We'd lived on the edge of the forest my entire life. Dad had been the first person I knew to break the rules; it had shocked the hell out of me when I saw him walking out of the woods with three hares on a pole across his shoulder. "Dad, I thought we weren't allowed to enter the woods?"

Our society had hammered that point into us, from before we were even able to speak. Images of the trees with a big red X painted across them. Not that anyone believed the reason why.

Dad took me into the trees the very next day, teaching me all the paths and trails. "If you look here, you can see where the mosses grow. So if you ever get turned around, just make sure the moss is growing on the opposite side. If you keep that side of the trees to your back, you'll always be able to find your way out of the woods."

I never thought to ask who had made those paths. When a place is forbidden, some people are always going to go and check it out for themselves. He took me to one of the rings too. "See the little stones, Kenny?"

I struggled not to giggle. The slabs were at least twelve feet high. Even the smallest ones were three feet across.

He heard me though. "It's not a laughing matter, son. We live in fear of them, that's why they tell us not to enter the forest. If the others knew the truth, they'd tell us everything. It's safe to be here during the day. Just be out before sunset, that's all. And never, no matter how tempted you are, go near the portal."

Dad showed me where that was too, a towering circle of stones, at least a hundred feet high. I couldn't fathom how the thing didn't just blow over in a high wind.

"It's held together by magic, Kenny. That's all you need to know, son. That and to never be here after dark, okay?"

I wish I had listened to the old man now.

* * *

Like I said before, I knew all the trails. Pretty much nothing in these woods scared me, perhaps the odd forgotten bear trap. Apart from those, there was little in this area that was going to surprise me.

Or so I thought.

Until that almost blinding flash of white light.

At first, I thought it was a freak lightning strike, so I made sure to get away from the trees, diving into the nearest clearing. Right into the path of . . .

Well, I had read enough fantasy stories to recognize a troll when I saw one.

Even when you've been warned about them, you generally don't expect to meet a walking pile of stones. Or three.

The second I saw them, I realized what my father had taken me to see when I was young. *The remains of a troll.* As I got to my feet, I realized the one in front of me wasn't alone. I blinked a few times just to make sure. Yep, there were three of them.

They reacted way faster than you'd think possible from creatures made of actual stone. Since the moment I'd seen the first one, I'd been looking for a way past. Two seconds, maybe three.

More than enough time for the closest troll to bend down, reach out and grab me.

"Don't squish him! We need him!"

Now, you'd think that a twenty-foot-tall pile of stones couldn't help but damage something like me, but I couldn't have been any more wrong. It held my wrist in its hand, hard enough that I couldn't escape but not so tight as to hurt me. To do that, it had to bend its knees and lean over at the waist too, so it was probably as uncomfortable for it to hold me as it was to have my arm held up at full stretch.

With its free hand, it scooped under my feet and lifted me up to its eye-line. Then the biggest of the group thundered over to us. "You, man?"

I nodded. "Yes. I'm a man. What do you want with me? I thought trolls didn't eat people?"

The myths and legends hadn't been particularly exact on that matter. Heck, they downright happily contradicted each other for all they were worth, in fact.

"Not always. You know woods?"

Again, I nodded. I figured the trolls could see fine in the dark. I could just about make out its body in what little light the stars offered. "Yes, I know the woods. You need help getting somewhere? I can do that, if you let me go when we get there."

"Stone circle, about this high?" It held its hand just above its head. They had come through the portal then? So that damn thing actually worked? I'd always thought that was just a damn fairy story Dad told to make me to go to sleep.

"You mean the portal? Yes, it's not that far from here. I can take you. You'll let me go then, yes?"

When the troll nodded its head, I expected the sound of stone grinding against stone, like an avalanche. But it was completely silent.

The one holding me up carefully set me back on the ground but kept its other hand around my wrist "You take us home now, okay?"

So off we went. Kenny McKinley and three bloody enormous trolls.

* * *

The shortest distance between two points is a straight line. It's worth reminding you of that. Oh, and that I wasn't sure if trolls ate people or not. Or if they kept their promises either.

Hi. I'm Kenny, and I'm a devious, unreliable bastard. *Just saying.*

Where they had caught me was less than ten minutes from the portal by the shortest path. There were no straight lines in the woods. Trees exist, that's why they are called the woods.

When Dad had taken me to see the remains of the troll, he'd explained how it came to be there. "You see, Kenny. The thing is, trolls can only survive over here in the dark. The second the sun rises, they're dead. They set, like concrete—rock solid. That one there, it eventually fell apart, as you see it now. Feet, legs, torso, neck, head, and arms. This might save your life one day, if you can keep a troll here until morning, you'll survive the encounter."

That memory had played back in my mind, from the moment the troll grabbed me.

Now, I could have taken them directly to the portal and hoped they let me go.

You know that's not what happened though. Like I just said, one of those trolls had grabbed a deer, thinking they could eat it. Which they probably could have. I'm no expert on trolls. I only lied to them because I figured if they knew they could eat animal flesh, they'd realize human flesh wasn't much different.

I started leading them through the woods. Using what little light I had from the occasional glimpse of the moon and ambient stars, I kept them on a circuit I used to walk in my youth, back after Dad passed away. I could almost hear his voice in the back of my mind as we went. "That's it, Kenny. Lead those stony bastards a merry dance. You'll see another day yet, son. Mark my words!"

When they had caught me, it had been just after midnight. At that time of year, sunrise was a little after six.

So I led them on a five-mile lap around the woods, diverting little more than a few feet on either side of our line, just to ensure they didn't get too familiar with our path. I knew the woods, even at this level of darkness. Anyone who hadn't spent years walking around would struggle to recognise one patch of trees from another. I was being cautious, ensuring the portal remained well out of our eyeline. It'd stay hidden behind the tallest trees until I wanted them to see it.

It became clear to me that these trolls hadn't crossed through the portal before. Anyone who'd been in these woods more than a few times, soon worked out where the stone circle was. In daylight, it was easy to see part of the outline from most paths through the trees. At night though? Not so much. Not at all, in fact.

I had to be careful, so they didn't get wise to the fact I was currently leading them in circles.

It worked fine, for about five hours. I could see from the sky that dawn wasn't far off, and so could they.

I'd forced the trolls to allow me a longer break from walking. They weren't big on sitting down or resting. One of them, in its frustration, leaned against a tree, uprooting the damn thing. I had to bite the insides of my cheeks to stop myself from laughing aloud as the beast smashed into the ground.

Then I realized, we couldn't come back this way again, or near it. It would be too obvious I had been walking them in circles, of course, if they'd spotted something like a recently downed tree, especially when one of them had recently knocked one over.

* * *

So as we walked, I began to move to my right, a few paces to the side for every step forward. I needed to make sure we weren't going to retrace our steps exactly this loop, as we'd been doing for the last five hours.

I think I got us about ten feet away from the trail we had been walking along.

Trolls aren't massively clever creatures. They aren't completely stupid either. They knew dawn wasn't far off and had been pushing me to walk faster. So we made that lap a little faster than the others.

Then they saw it. *Well, their leader did.*

I could almost see the thought process running through its mind.

The thing is, the troll who'd been holding my forearm had been careful. It had been holding me with the lightest possible grip. Those trolls weren't stupid, they knew I was the only way they'd find the portal. All those trails looked the same.

Apart from a recently pushed over tree.

When their leader shouted, the troll holding me reacted in the strangest way. I don't know if it had worked out what I was doing and why, or if it just had a death wish. The damn thing let me go.

At precisely two minutes to sunrise.

I just ran full pelt along the closest track away from the portal. They saw the portal about two seconds later.

It felt like a small earthquake, so I looked over my shoulder for half a second. The leader and the troll who'd been holding me were running for the portal. The one who'd knocked down the tree was... trying to chase me?

What the actual fuck was it thinking?

All three of them must have seen how close they were to the portal, so why had that one decided to chase me? There was no possible way it was going to be able to catch me and get back through the portal before the sun came up.

The instant I knew I was being chased, I started making it tougher to follow me, dodging through the thickest patches of trees in front of me.

That's probably what saved my life, looking back now.

That and the cedar tree. It was the one tree Dad had always told me to be aware of. Somewhere in the long distant past, somebody had used stones to make the trunk grow a hollow spot. I knew how big the troll's hands were—he wouldn't be able to get at me—and dived inside.

Not that it mattered.

From my bolthole, I saw the troll who'd been holding me barely make it through the portal. I realized then, where the white flash had come from. Another flash emitted from the stone circle just as dawn broke. Then I saw a boulder the size of my head hit the ground. The creature had lost its foot as the portal closed.

Their leader didn't make it into the portal. It set solid as the sun hit it, mere inches away. As for my pursuer? Well, he was never going to catch anyone now.

* * *

Fast forward sixty years. Here I now stand before you, Ranger Kenny McKinley. "Welcome to the wildlife tour of Auburn Forest. This," I pointed to a pile of stones, "and that over there, are trolls. It's okay, they're both quite dead. That's the reason you're forbidden to enter this forest after dark. If you want to take a seat on old stony's leg there, I'll explain exactly how they got here... "

The Waiting Tree

Eric Fritz

The first time Josh heard about the dating tree it sounded like a joke. Kimi leaned down the bar to yell over Brett's latest relationship complaints.

"Apps are so trashy now. You should put a letter in that tree in the park."

It came out that all of them had heard of this tree. It was an old oak with a hollow in the middle where people dropped personal ads. You could read through other people's letters and respond to the ones you liked.

"It sounds so much more personal," Kimi said over the top of her beer. "It's not just swiping, you have to really say something."

Josh left before they ordered the next round, but he couldn't stop wondering if it was real. Second year residency in a hospital didn't leave time for anything besides work and paperwork. Drinks with the other residents were the only social event he got, and a few attempts to set up dates online always ran into scheduling issues.

He could have tried to date someone at work, but watching Zack and Sarah date and break up and date and just be friends and maybe hook up was exhausting. There was no way he was going to make the mistake of getting involved with a coworker, but it was so hard to find someone else who understood how little time residents had.

The next day after his shift Josh walked to the park still wearing his scrubs. He felt stupid even considering it, but the idea of meeting someone was too alluring to pass up.

The park was mostly empty and it was easy to spot the tree. The old oak was set off by itself in the far corner. It still towered above the other trees spread around the park.

Nothing looked special about it as he approached. Josh started to think it was a prank until he got close enough to see into the hollow. It was stuffed with envelopes and folded papers in all different colors.

He pulled out a few at random. They all had different collections of symbols or obvious pseudonyms. He recognized the male and female symbols, as well as a few combinations, but there were others he had no idea about.

None of the ones with symbols were sealed, and all of them seemed to follow a pattern of talking about themselves, talking about what they wanted, and being signed with a made-up name.

Seeing so many letters was overwhelming. He stuffed them all back and sat down to write his own, leaning against the tree and using his messenger bag as a writing desk.

It was pretty easy to talk about himself. Great student, doctor, passable cook. It was much harder to talk about what he wanted. Did he want to meet someone who was cute? Funny? He settled for a good conversationalist.

Thinking of a pseudonym for the signature was also a challenge. Was something with doctor in it too obvious? Professor Morgan, in college, had always complained about the caduceus being mistaken for the medical symbol, which was really the Rod of Asclepius. So he signed Asclepius-in-Anticipation, folded the letter up before he could change his mind, and tucked it in between a large pink envelope and a smaller yellow one.

It was two days before he could make it back to the park. There must have been fifty letters jammed into the tree; he flipped through each one, until he finally caught sight of one with his pseudonym on the outside. However, the anticipation quickly turned into disappointment when he realized it was a generic welcome letter explaining the rules.

One letter at a time, no watching the tree to see who else came, it all seemed pretty basic.

On the back was a list of the different symbols people used. Some were easy to guess but some of the others surprised him. Apparently, the heart with an infinity symbol twisted through it was for polyamorous relationships.

He tucked the card into his bag, wondering who had time to hand write these and address them to every new person.

The next few times he stopped by there was nothing new, but he remembered his mother saying *you have to send mail to get mail* when he was young.

On the next sunny day, he showed up with paper and envelopes and sat down against the tree. There were two letters that caught his eye.

To *lonely-in-the-dark* he wrote about working night shifts, being up late, and listening to Chopin pieces.

To *straight-up-change-up* he wrote about some of the things he'd cooked, although it was mostly back in college.

It was four days before he made it back to check, and there was one letter from *straight-up*. Her name was Melissa and she was mostly interested in the Red Sox and going to the gym.

He was in the hospital cafeteria and still puzzling over what to write when Brett dropped a tray on the table and sat down across from him.

"You get a foreign pen pal?"

Josh looked up. "What? Oh, no. It's from that tree that Kimi was talking about."

"The dating tree?" Brett laughed. "Might as well just put a want ad in the newspaper, if anyone still reads them."

"I don't know, it seems fun." Josh shrugged. "I don't know what to write back to this woman though."

"What's her deal?"

"Sports and the gym, I guess. She mentioned something about liking whiskey."

"Tell her you work out." Brett glanced down at his arms and back. "Maybe you should start hitting the gym anyway."

Josh crossed his arms. "In all of my copious free time, sure."

Brett laughed. "Man, just tell her you're sensitive and you can cook."

Josh laughed too, but he took a little of Brett's advice along with throwing in some more about his favorite musical pieces.

Her second reply was just a few sentences long. He tried to think of something more interesting to say, but he wasn't surprised when a week passed and there was no third reply.

Another week passed before he made it back. The weather was beautiful and he had plenty of time to look through the letters, but the only one that caught his eye was from a man. He was a med student at a nearby college who liked jazz and Russian literature.

Josh wasn't sure why he opened it in the first place, other than that he'd been trying to figure out how other people did this. It wasn't that he'd never considered the idea, he just never really knew where to begin. He scribbled a quick reply and tucked it into the tree before hurrying home.

To his surprise, the next day there were two letters addressed to him. One from the med student, and another he didn't recognize. The med student's letter was nice, but immediately suggested meeting in person for coffee.

The other one was folded around something rectangular that turned out to be a polaroid of a man from shoulders to knees, completely naked. Josh swallowed hard. It wasn't that it looked bad, whoever was in the photo was in great shape, but it was just too much.

Face burning, he crumpled both letters up and tossed them in the trash can at the edge of the park.

The time between trips to the park grew further apart. There was nothing for him in the tree, and it was hard to find the time to get away from work.

On his third trip with no results something made him stop.

He'd looked through every letter, and his original one wasn't there. Something tickled the back of his mind. In order to keep things fresh old letters were eventually taken out, so you'd need to write a new one every few months.

That was fine, it wasn't that hard to think of some new things to say. But pulling a blank piece of paper out of his bag stopped him dead. What could he say now that he hadn't said in the first letter?

The white sheet of paper filled his vision until his eyes grew misty. He rubbed the back of his wrist against his eyes, scribbled "*Why is this so hard?*" onto the paper, and jammed it into the tree.

He probably never would have gone back if it hadn't come up again at the bar.

"Oh yeah, Josh was putting letters in it," Brett slurred over a pint of beer a few weeks later.

"No way." Zack laughed.

Sarah swatted his arm. "Be nice." She turned towards him. "Tell us about it, Joshua."

He glanced around the table, suddenly uncomfortable. "I dunno, it sounded fun when Kimi talked about it, but it didn't really go anywhere."

"That's cool you actually tried it." Kimi smiled. "I just heard people talk about it in town, I've never even been there."

"You don't think it's weird?"

"No way," Zack said. "I'd try it." He looked at Sarah and quickly added, "If I was single, I mean."

"Yeah man." Brett thumped his shoulder slightly too hard. "Don't give up. It's no weirder than online dating."

The next day Josh trekked back out to the park. It didn't seem likely that anything would have shown up after all this time, but he was amazed to find a folded piece of paper with his pseudonym on the outside, written in a large swoopy hand.

It was the same piece of paper he'd written his question on, but underneath it someone had replied. *You have a kind soul. I'd like to hear more about you.*

There was no signature or anything to indicate who had written it and why they'd waited so long. Josh wrote a few sentences about a medical case he was puzzling over at work, no personal details obviously, and put it back in the tree.

Over the next few weeks there was a new letter every time he stopped by the tree. He still didn't know the person's name, gender, or anything else about them; but each letter got longer and longer as he poured out more about his life. It didn't seem to matter how he addressed them either, the same person always found them. He got to recognize their handwriting instantly.

"This is the happiest I've seen you in months," Kimi remarked one day in the break room.

Josh looked up from a letter he was working on and smiled. "It's nice to be able to connect with someone."

The letters were a strange mix of anecdotes, observations, and historical information. Some of it had to be made up, how could anyone know what happened in that park a hundred years ago? But the few things he was able to look up all seemed accurate.

It was on a whim one day that he looked up "can trees talk" online and ended up at a website about Dryads. They were mythological spirits that lived in trees, and were supposedly very shy.

He wrote the question as a joke at the end of his next letter, hoping it would prompt his mysterious correspondent to say something about themselves.

There was no letter the next day, and on the following day he found an envelope addressed to him in a short, blocky script. When he turned it over to open it, the words *I'm sorry* were written in that familiar flowing handwriting.

He opened the envelope carefully, making sure not to tear the part with writing on it.

The letter was dated from weeks ago. It must have been written just after the correspondence with the mysterious writer started. She was interested in classical music and literature, and seemed to have a lot to say. It was the kind of thing he'd have loved to get in the beginning, but something about it just didn't feel right anymore.

He held up the part of the envelope that read *I'm sorry*, turning it back and forth in the sunlight. The ink wasn't quite black, but a shade of dark brown or red; the kind of thing someone might make from nuts or berries if they couldn't get real ink. That couldn't be, though, could it?

Whoever he'd been writing to for all these weeks, they were something really special. He'd rather keep talking to them than anyone else.

He crumpled the letter and jammed it into his bag to toss later, then sat down with his back against the tree to write. It must have been his imagination, but it almost felt like someone rested a hand on his shoulder.

One with the Forest

Kevin Hopson

"Are you okay?" Modrad asked.

He watched as Farfiz put a hand to the tree, leaning against it. The gnome huffed, then bent over and coughed. Modrad couldn't see much with Farfiz's back to him. A spattering noise followed, much like the sound of rain pelting dry leaves. An upset stomach perhaps.

"I'm going to assume you're not," Modrad said.

Farfiz turned to him, his face pale and clammy. Normally known for his pranks and playfulness, Farfiz hardly resembled the troublemaker Modrad had grown accustomed to.

Dwarves were a stubborn race. They didn't always get along with others, especially mischievous gnomes, but Modrad had developed a bond with Farfiz ever since the day they met. He'd admit that Farfiz annoyed him at times, but Modrad felt a genuine sense of concern for his friend.

Modrad approached Farfiz and extended a hand. Farfiz gripped it.

"Maybe you should sit down," Modrad said.

He wrapped an arm around the back of Farfiz's waist, gently

lowering him to the ground. Farfiz sat with his back to the tree, his breathing still labored.

"What is it?" Modrad asked.

Farfiz shook his head and pursed his lips. He surveyed the woodlands. "The forest," he finally said. "It's under attack."

The forest was Farfiz's home, and he had a spiritual connection to it. If something was out of tune, he felt it. Literally.

"Water," Farfiz said.

"What?"

"Do you have any water?"

"My waterskin is dry," Modrad replied.

"There's a stream just west of here," Farfiz said, pointing. "It should only take you a few minutes."

"No problem," Modrad said. He glanced west, then turned his attention to Farfiz. "Are you sure you'll be okay?"

Farfiz managed to shrug, a slight grin stretching across his face. Modrad took some comfort in that. His friend wasn't too far gone. Farfiz coughed again, and Modrad took that as a sign to get moving.

"I'll be back shortly," Modrad said.

Modrad headed west, settling into a brisk walk. He scanned the forest canopy. Normally, the treetops weren't dense enough to block out the sun, but something was turning back the morning light.

A slight glow emanated from above, surrounded by various shades of gray. Fog? No. It was definitely something else. Something more ominous. And when Modrad finally caught a whiff, the answer became clear. Smoke.

Modrad picked up the pace, dead leaves and twigs crackling beneath his boots as he worked his way into a jog. Then his right foot sunk, throwing him off balance. Modrad tumbled to the ground, his hands helping to break the fall.

He let out a moan and rolled over on his back. Modrad sat up, sifting debris from his beard. He squinted at the hole in the distance, cursing the rabbit that made it. But he quickly swallowed his anger.

"Sorry, my friend," he whispered to the rabbit hole. "It's no fault of your own. I just need to watch where I'm going."

Modrad got to his feet, but his ankle nearly buckled under the weight. He winced and took a moment to gather himself. Modrad put some weight on the ankle, grinding his teeth to fight back the pain. But he didn't have a choice. He had to keep going.

Though he could no longer jog, Modrad managed to limp along at a decent pace. He glanced down at his belt. Thankfully, the waterskin was still there. Finding the stream wouldn't do much good without it.

He spotted a clearing up ahead, a trail of smoke rising from a nearby campfire. Modrad slowed his pace. He heard voices in the distance. Then something disturbing caught his eye. It wasn't a natural clearing. The trees had been cut, and several piles of logs lined one side of the clearing.

That wasn't the worst of it, though. Three wolves hung from a low tree branch. The meat of the animals remained, but their fur was gone.

Modrad put a hand over his shoulder. Slung along his back was a battle axe. He gripped the top of the handle and slid it from its leather sleeve. Modrad didn't want to give the impression of being an aggressor, but the situation warranted caution.

"Who are you?" a voice said.

Modrad spun around. A burly, bare-chested man stared back at him, holding a hatchet at his side. Modrad tightened his grip on the axe.

"Looks like we have a visitor," another voice said.

Modrad glanced over his shoulder, and two other men approached. They were fully clothed, unlike the third man, but looked just as muscular. The three men spread out, effectively forming a triangle around Modrad.

"A dwarf of all things," the third man said. The men laughed in unison. "And he has a weapon."

"So do I," the shirtless man said. "How much do you think we can fetch for him?"

Modrad sensed that tensions were building, and his only way out would be to fight. Words wouldn't make much difference with these men. He'd fought tougher adversaries. Even dragons on a few occasions. But he had allies in those situations. And a lot of luck to go along with it. Modrad never balked at a fight, but he had to admit the odds were against him, especially with a lame ankle.

"He's mine," the shirtless man said.

Modrad pivoted his feet so he wasn't facing any of the men head on. He preferred to keep all three of them in his line of sight, and the only way to do that was by using his peripheral vision. Modrad switched the axe to his left hand. It wasn't his dominant hand, but the shirtless man to Modrad's left seemed to pose the biggest threat. If the other two decided to get involved, at least he'd have a free hand to try and hold them off.

The shirtless man made his move. He walked very methodically toward Modrad, hatchet in hand. The other two followed suit, but they slowed and kept their distance, granting their friend the one-on-one opportunity he desired.

Without warning, the shirtless man rushed Modrad, and the dwarf raised the blade of the axe above his shoulder. Modrad's blade was much larger than that of the hatchet, but he knew speed and agility could trump a larger weapon.

With the man almost in range, Modrad readied the axe. He was about to bring the axe down on him, but the man surprised Modrad. His adversary dropped and slid along the ground, clearing the handle of the axe and taking Modrad's feet out from under him.

Modrad collapsed onto his stomach, the axe dislodging from his hand. The impact knocked the air from his lungs, and Modrad struggled to catch his breath.

Before he could reach for the axe, Modrad felt something hard and heavy against his back. It wasn't the hatchet. It was the man's knee. The shirtless man was holding him down, all of his weight digging deep into Modrad's back. Modrad let out a grunt.

If the man was planning on killing Modrad, it was the ideal time to do it. But he'd mentioned fetching a price for the dwarf earlier. If that was the case, the men needed him alive. Modrad didn't know why, and he didn't care to ponder. But if he had to wager a guess, Modrad assumed he would be sold to someone looking for slave labor.

Modrad would rather die fighting than face that fate but, as much as he tried, he couldn't muster a defense. The man was twice his size and had all of the leverage. Modrad heard a growl to his left. And then a blur of gray.

Almost immediately, the weight had been lifted from his back. Screams followed. Modrad grasped his axe and turned to look. Two of the men were retreating into thicker woods, several wolves in pursuit of them. The shirtless man, meanwhile, lay on his back with a wolf on top of him.

"Enough," a voice said.

Modrad's eyes bulged. It was Farfiz.

The wolf backed away, and Modrad noticed the man's hatchet on the ground. He bent over and clutched it with his free hand, making certain it wouldn't be used against them. Farfiz sidled up to him. The gnome panted, and Modrad did the same.

"As usual," Modrad said. "Your timing is impeccable."

Farfiz had saved Modrad's hide more times than he could remember. Much of it was due to the gnome's special ability. Through his connection with nature, he could will animals to do his bidding.

"I smelled the smoke," Farfiz said, hunched over with hands on his knees. "I thought you might be in trouble."

"I can't believe you made it this far."

"It took every ounce of energy I had," Farfiz replied. "Thankfully, I managed to summon the wolves just in time."

Modrad glimpsed the encampment, hoping that Farfiz wouldn't notice the wolves dangling from the tree. "You don't want to see the carnage."

"I don't have to," Farfiz said. "I can sense it." He looked to the shirtless man. "You'll leave these woods and never come back. Otherwise, you'll meet a much worse fate. Go tell your friends the same. Assuming they're still alive."

The man showed no signs of compassion. He only offered a stern face. Then he got to his feet and walked away, looking over his shoulder to make sure no one or no thing was in pursuit.

Farfiz fell to one knee. Modrad dropped the two blades and came to his friend's aid. He placed both hands under Farfiz's armpits and pulled him toward a tree, wincing briefly as his ankle flared. The gnome sat against the tree, and Modrad retrieved the blades. He sheathed the battle axe and handed the hatchet to Farfiz.

"Stay here this time," Modrad said. "The wolf can keep you company."

Farfiz managed to nod.

"I'll be back with that water."

Modrad set out for the stream, limping along just as before. The stinging in his ankle gradually turned to an aching sensation as he pressed on, making the trek a little more manageable. Modrad passed the encampment along the way.

It pained him to see the butchery the men had inflicted upon the forest and its animals, but Modrad knew the healing process could begin now that the men were gone. It would take some time for the forest to recover. And, in the process, Farfiz as well.

He heard a trickling of water nearby and followed the sound, reaching the stream only seconds later. Modrad grabbed the waterskin from a hook along his belt and pulled the top free. He knelt along the bank and lowered the container into the water.

His eyes widened. The water was tinted red. Modrad emptied the waterskin and moved it to a clearer patch of water, filling it to the top. Perhaps there was a dead animal upstream. It would explain the strange color if the animal was bleeding out.

But part of him couldn't help but feel unsettled. As if something sinister was at work in these woods. Something worse than the men he encountered. Modrad shrugged it off. He needed to get back to Farfiz.

With the waterskin secure, Modrad got to his feet and turned to walk. He glanced over his shoulder one last time, eyeing the stream. For the sake of his friend, he hoped the forest was truly on the mend.

The Birthday Tree

Adam Meyer

Every year, just as winter faded and spring began to bloom, Kevin watched his mother grow sad again. He'd often find her moping around the house, her heavy shoes scuffing the hardwood floors, her lips pressed down at the corners. Once in a while he'd spot her staring out the parlor window at the tall oak tree squatting in the front yard, her eyes as wide as the delicate saucers in the breakfront, and have the sense she'd been there for hours. He knew why she was sad, only there was nothing he could do about it.

The problem was his birthday.

It should've been a celebration, a happy time. But his mother never gave him any presents. She did always make a cake for him—chocolate with cream cheese frosting, his favorite—but it was usually overcooked and dry as dust, and he swore he could taste the tears mixed in with the batter.

Kevin had grown to hate his birthday.

"Maybe we should just forget it this year," he told his mother a couple years ago, when he found her staring at an old photo album.

The yellowed pages were spread across her lap, her fingers tracing the images like letters on a tombstone. "My birthday, I mean."

"Wouldn't matter. That day'll come one way or the other." She closed the book and looked at him. "Besides, it's not right for a boy to ignore his birthday."

He nodded, thinking that was true. Only they both knew a boy who didn't have a birthday, at least not anymore. Colin.

Kevin felt guilty that he could barely remember him. He held tightly to a distant memory of being in their bedroom together, toy trucks sprawled on the floor between them, pushing them back and forth on wobbly plastic wheels. He could recall being on his mother's lap, him on one knee, Colin on the other, the scent of woodsmoke rising to his nostrils as she sang an old folk song. And most of all he could remember that day he and Colin had climbed the old oak tree out front, him looking up through a screen of branches as Colin climbed, higher and higher, shouting, "Look at me, look at me." Kevin had tried to glance over, but he was too busy trying to hang on himself, when he heard a sharp grrrrack! and a scream. Then he did look, and there was Colin, crashing through the branches, hurtling toward the ground.

Three days later Colin was dead.

He passed away just after midnight, a few minutes into what would have been their sixth birthday. They were supposed to have some of their friends from school over to play games and have cake—half chocolate and half vanilla in those days, because the boys could never agree on a flavor—but of course his mother had canceled the celebration on account of what happened. Kevin never did have another party, and he rarely got invited to any, either. He hated birthdays and couldn't wait until his own was just a distant memory.

Only one more day to go.

The evening of his sixteenth birthday, he sat on the front porch, lulled by the sound of the whispering grass, staring into the blue-gray dusk. He was supposed to be doing his homework, but he couldn't seem to make himself move. He just stared at the old oak tree and its web of black branches, tiny white blossoms tucked into the shadowy corners, and wondered for the millionth time what his life would be like if Colin hadn't lost hold of that upper branch, if his brother were here to celebrate his birthday—their birthday.

Sometimes, when he had this thought, he could almost feel Colin out there in the yellow-green fields, hear his voice on the light breeze that tickled the hairs just above his spine. '*Colin*,' he'd think, or maybe he'd even say it out loud. "Colin, come back to us."

But, of course, he never did.

That night Kevin and his mother ate dinner without saying a word, the silence even heavier than usual. They had beef stew, which had been Colin's favorite, although Kevin preferred chicken. He found the meat dry and chewy and pushed it around his plate, choking down as much as he could. When he was done, he brought his dishes to the sink and looked back at his mother. She'd barely even touched her food.

"Let me help wash up, Mom."

"No, you're the birthday boy... "

"Not until tomorrow."

She shook her head, tears glistening in the corners of her eyes. "Go on, I'll handle it."

Kevin ignored the faint sound of her crying as he trudged up the stairs. He lay in his bed, studying the bookshelf that hugged the far wall. Scratches in the hardwood marked the place where Colin's narrow bed used to be. Kevin lay down fully-dressed on his own mattress and shut his eyes, feeling the warmth of his tears.

He must've fallen asleep, because when Kevin sat up again, he felt groggy and out-of-sorts. A glance at the bedside clock told him it was eleven-fifty-five, just a few minutes until his birthday.

Instead of just lying there and letting himself be paralyzed by memories, he found himself standing, slipping his shoes on, tiptoeing quietly down the stairs. His mother was asleep in a chair in the parlor, snoring gently. He opened the front door with glacial slowness, fearing the screech of the old hinges would wake her. But they didn't.

The grass was wet with dew and the moon shone like a bright white beacon overhead. Kevin went to the oak tree and, for the first time since his brother's fall, reached up for the lowest branch. He used his feet to get purchase against the rough bark and hauled himself up. Climbing was easier than he remembered. He reached from one branch to another, pulling himself higher and higher, until he found a long sturdy perch on which to rest. He put one hand on the trunk, balancing easily. Feeling the cool night air sear his lungs, he looked back at the dark house from which he had come.

Above him, shadows stirred and leaves rustled.

Kevin tensed, gripping the branch below him so tightly that the rough bark burned his fingers. He took in ragged breaths, his eyes straining to make out shapes in the patchwork of shadows above.

Something was moving through the branches, coming right for him.

"Who's there?" he called, feeling his whole body tense as he looked up, the moon's bloated white belly showing through bare leaves. He angled forward, trying to get a better look at the small, dark figure that lunged from branch to branch, but he couldn't quite make it out. Then he saw four small, white fingers curling like worms around the limb above. Tilting his head back further, he spotted a nest of dark hair.

A boy plunged down through the leaves, crouching on the same branch on which Kevin was resting.

The small round face was instantly familiar from old photos. It had been his own face once.

"Colin," he said.

"How do you know my name?" the boy asked, cocking his head slightly.

He found the words sticking in his throat like the too-dry stew he'd pushed around his dinner plate. "Because you're my brother. I'm Kevin."

The deep brown eyes went wide, his innocent face scrunching in concentration. "You can't be. You're big."

"That's because... " Kevin couldn't say it. He was afraid that if he did, he would break the spell and Colin would vanish. Instead, he said, "Happy birthday."

"It's my birthday?"

"Our birthday."

"How old am I then? Six?"

For a long moment, Kevin couldn't seem to answer. "Yes, you're six... I'm older."

"But I thought we were the same age."

"We are. I mean, we used to be. We... "

"It's our birthday!"

As Colin swung his legs over the branch that held them, Kevin felt his stomach lurch. But Colin was firmly in control as he spun toward the trunk and grabbed on. He slid down as if on a fireman's pole, finding his footing on another branch, one that shook a little beneath his weight. Reaching out toward him Kevin shouted, "Hold on, be careful!" but Colin didn't listen. He just reached out, hooking his tiny fists on another offshoot, swinging down.

"Hooray, it's my birthday!"

"Wait, come back... "

Kevin scaled awkwardly onto the next branch, looking down, but the weave of shadows was thick and all he could see was his brother disappearing through a patchwork of leaves, running toward the house.

"Colin! Please!"

For a moment Kevin stood there, clutching the branch, and then he began to make his way down the tree quickly, moving from one branch to another, shifting his weight carefully. Soon the ground was there, maybe fifteen feet below him now, and he hung on tight, careful not to slip. He eased one leg free, then the other, hanging on by just his hands.

When he hit the dirt, he was out of breath and his head was pounding slightly.

Colin, he thought, racing for the house.

As he got inside, however, there was no sign of his brother. His mother was still snoring gently in the old armchair, and the air was heavy with the smell of charred meat. He looked through all the first-floor rooms, but they were empty. Then he headed upstairs, and looked in the spare room, his mother's room, and finally his own.

It was just his imagination. Colin hadn't been there. His mind had tricked him. Colin was gone.

The knowledge of this—both so deeply ingrained and yet shockingly new—felt as heavy around his shoulders as a scarf made of stones. He looked out the window at the old oak tree, its branches spiderwebbing into the dark, studying every shadow for some trace of Colin. Finding none, he turned back to the bed, his mind fuzzy, his muscles worn. He lay down on his bed, exhausted.

He woke a short time later, aches moving through his body, especially his right leg and lower back, a screaming headache piercing his head. He tried to open his eyes but his vision swam, and when he finally saw his mother there she seemed younger than he remembered, her deeply grooved face as smooth as stone.

"Oh Colin," she said, and he tried to tell her— my name's not Colin, I'm Kevin, I'm alive. "Don't leave me," she went on, "don't you dare!"

I'm not going anywhere, he thought. Then another face swam into his vision, it was Colin again. His dark eyes twinkled, his mouth pushing up at the corners.

"Happy birthday, Colin," he said.

"But I'm not... " Kevin said, or tried to say. His thoughts got foggy; darkness began to cloud his vision. He reached out for something to hold onto, something to tether him to this world, but pain shot up his arm and his fingers closed on air, and soon there was no darkness, no pain, nothing left at all.

Rooted in My Next Life

Daniel Klim

I never believed in reincarnation.

See, in my last life, it never clicked with me. I do good things or bad things, and the balance between the two determines what I am in my next life? It was stupid to me. No reason to it. Nonsensical. “God, was I - sorry. *Universe*, was I wrong.”

* * *

My first day of my new life was very different from my last life—when I was human. This go around, I peeked out of something dusty and stared into the sun. I felt only grass and dirt around me, touching my face.

Face. We’ll get to that later.

My view was strictly the blue sky above me, with the occasional bright, white cloud passing by. I’ll admit, I was dying to see some action. I couldn’t tell if it was Heaven or some kind of purgatory. Granted, it was as boring as you could imagine. The only interesting thing that happened was that it would get darker and the sun would leave. Then it became black and you could see the moon. Insane, right?

The weird thing was, the sun and moon were the only things I could remember from my past life. Seeing the two alternate above me reminded me of these vague, yet familiar, memories from my past life. I remember there being a sun and moon back then, too. It's hard to explain.

It's hard to look at the sun and moon all day, too.

After the first couple of days, I noticed I was slowly coming out of the ground. Below me, I could see grass and, a little to my right, I saw what appeared to be an oak tree. Just a small sapling. A light wind was making us sway. I tried looking around to get a sense of where I was, but could only see the grass and the oak tree. This went on for a couple of weeks.

After settling on this view for now, I realized something about the afterlife. I can only think about what's in front of me if it is something that I can remember from my past life. The first day, I saw the sun and knew what it was. During the night, I saw the moon and could recognize it. I couldn't recall what an oak tree was, however, until I saw one beside me a few weeks later. The same thing happened this morning.

I was gazing into the grass and oak tree, my usual view for now, and felt a soft, wet sensation touching onto me. It got heavier and heavier for a while, then died down.

Rain.

Glorious rain. Now I recognized the rain and it felt good on me. Universe, it felt *great* on me. Better than the sun and the wind. My initial thoughts were justified now. I can only identify something from my past life if it's unfolding in front of me. There it is.

This revelation calmed me down. Now, all I had to do was wait and I would eventually piece together exactly where I was. It felt more like Heaven than Hell, but, then again, I'm only a couple of weeks old. I'll have to wait and see what's really going on.

For the next couple of months, it was the same cycle of sun, moon, and rain with grass and my oak tree friend next to me. But everything changed on a particularly gray-skied day.

In my peripheral vision, I could see a branch coming out of me. An oak tree branch. I swear to the Universe, it was coming directly out of me. My "eyes" were still stuck, positioned to only see what's in front of me. This was my only sign of any claimable appendage. At that moment, it clicked with me.

I'm a tree.

I'm really a *tree.*

An oak tree with another oak tree right next to me. Great.

Panic settled in and I tried moving, but I felt my roots trying to tug around inside the Earth. Nothing was happening. I tried to yell, but no sound came out. I tried moving my body, but it was a tree, for Universe's sake. My face was bark. Everything was. Within this episode of mine, I started to feel dizzy. Nothing felt real, but I was quickly proven wrong.

I suddenly saw my body from a third-person angle instead of my POV of nature. I saw myself as a tree, with branches slightly swinging back and forth. I saw many trees around me, and it was freaky to look at. Trees as far as the new angle would let me see. After a minute of this, I returned to my normal view and the dizziness was gone.

My epiphany ended, and my gaze into the grass felt more strained. More memories were coming back to me from what could only be my past life. I remember a blurry vision of myself as a person, running through woods similar to what I'm now a part of. I can now remember all different kinds of trees, and forests and leaves, all reminding me of my current state.

How could this happen?

No, *why* did this happen?

What in Universe's name did I do?

These were the only thoughts and revelations I had for years after that moment. Nothing new came for the rest of the year. And nothing in an entire year after that. And a couple years after that. No new action. Just the elements I was introduced to in my first couple of months of this new life, and what the epiphany brought. Nothing for so long.

* * *

It's easy to keep track of things when your life amounts to so little. It must have been a decade after that third-person view where everything clicked. It all looked the same, in case you were wondering.

All the trees around me got bigger and bigger. Now there were shadows on the grass and leaves falling sometimes. I would hear animal noises from birds and squirrels and be reminded of the vast forest from my previous life. With every new creature I heard jumping or crawling around, I would get a glimmer of something from my past. With every new creature I heard jumping or crawling around, I would get a glimmer of something from my past life with the forest.

But what did I do there? Was my whole life spent in the forest, too? I mean, honestly, was I a different kind of tree in my past life or something? Is that how it worked?

Maybe I was bad at being an evergreen tree. The Universe struck down and turned me into an oak tree for this life. It's all so stupid. Why can't everything just turn pitch black? I would have no conscience, and everything would be—well I don't know. I wouldn't be there. I wouldn't even know I'm dead. At the very least, I wouldn't be stuck as a tree for who knows how long.

Years of cycling through these thoughts made me feel crazy at first. After what must have been a million revolutions of the sun and moon, things felt final. My boring life as a tree seemed like it would go on forever. All I saw these past years were the same natural elements with no recollection of anything else from my past life.

Maybe that is Heaven, though. That which I *don't* remember. The absence of everything except all this nature. At the same time, it felt like Hell the way everything was so painfully slow and unexciting. Or maybe this could be a transitioning period. Like this is some gateway to—

RUH-RUH-RUH-RUH-RUH!

Holy Universe, this was not an animal sound. In front of me, the oak, proudly standing tall, was making the loudest noise I've ever heard, just at its bottom. I dropped my gaze a little further down and saw woodchips flying everywhere. At the base of the tree, a thin, spinning, metal plate was creating a line clean across the thing!

A million thoughts went rushing through my head and I finally got it. All my visions from my past life came back to me all at once, from when I was human and all the things I did then. It all came and struck me as I saw the destruction in front of me. Now I remembered, I used to call this a chainsaw.

I remembered it all now. In my past life, memories of me walking through the woods with that same kind of chainsaw. I was in a human body, in uniform, and sweating. I was cutting down every sturdy tree I saw with the chainsaw. I remember turning fully-grown oak trees into logs. And I would get paid for it.

It made sense now. I should have never done any of that. I wouldn't have done it if it meant this result. A life as a tree. Now I see someone doing the same exact thing. If only I could take it back, I swear I would. Anything to avoid whatever reincarnation this is now.

I want to get out of here.

The noise finished, and the tree came crashing down. A bearded man wearing the same exact uniform I had was towering over the stump, looking at the destruction. He looked around at all the other trees, then came to me. He looked me up and down. He slowly nodded. Then he stepped over the stump and moved up to me.

I need to get out of here.

That was my very last thought before I felt the sharp stinging of a thousand blades cutting through me.

Now it's just pitch-black and nothing.

Jodie's Spot

Mark Towse

The ring of fog looks other-worldly from the top of this hill, impossibly symmetrical and well-formed, and my mind wanders to all the wondrous possibilities capable of producing such a phenomenon. My parents say that I have an over-active imagination. It's better than not having one at all.

If Jodie were here right now, she would be bouncing up and down with anticipation. Her excited voice hangs in my head, "*What is it, Steve*?"

"I don't know, Sis," I whisper.

I've been walking for hours now. Blue skies have given way to matt dullness, and it's impossible to tell what time it is. Shrugging off the backpack, I unzip the front pocket and take a mouthful of the tepid water from the crumpled bottle. The pause in movement allows the cool air to wrap around me, goosebumps prickling my skin.

I like to lose myself in nature, become part of it, and I refuse to bring a watch or phone out with me. Mum and Dad used to insist, but not anymore, not now that it's just me.

It's a gamble, though. The car is a long way back, and I know I'd never find my way in the dark. Jodie would want to investigate, though. For her, I thread my arm through the strap of the pack and march on.

"This is for you, Jodie!"

I was sixteen when my sister went missing, just over a year ago now. I still struggle to accept that she's gone. Sometimes when I'm hiking, I think I see her, climbing a tree or scrambling down a rockface. But I know it can't be so.

She's here somewhere, though.

Always our favourite place, I think she used to love being out here even more than I did.

Since the day of her disappearance, I have been haunted by bad dreams. I guess Mum and Dad figure I'm old enough to deal with it. It sure doesn't feel that way. Besides, they have nothing to give.

And they don't look at me the same way anymore.

Occasional and distant whistles from the birds fill the air and break the hushed sound of my feet on the soft grass. The snap of a branch underfoot startles me, and I mock myself with a snigger. It is so quiet out here, exactly how I like it. That's how we both used to like it.

Nobody knew she was coming out that day. She never told a soul—left a note for Mum and Dad that she had gone to her friend Melissa's house. When she didn't return that night, they rang Melissa and uncovered the lie. It was me that checked her closet and found her hiking shoes and favourite backpack missing, the one I bought her the previous month for her fourteenth birthday.

The closer I get to the ring, the more I expect the magic at some point to fade and for the imperfections to show, but the mist isn't getting thinner or any less alluring. It's only a few feet away now, but it's impossible to see through, so dense and full of mystery.

I have never seen anything like it before.

Jodie would be in overdrive now, non-stop chattering about how awesome it was. Even now, as I draw up to its outside edge, it is no less impressive. Slowly, I raise my arm and plunge my hand into its smoky coldness. The illusion is quite spooky, my handless limb emerging from the grey vortex.

Tentatively, I step forward into the vapor-like wall. My body gives out a shudder as the iciness hits, and I'm immediately disoriented by the deafening silence and starkness that greets me. Regardless, I continue walking towards the center.

Visibility is poor, and I can't see the arm in front of me nor my legs beneath me. It's making me lightheaded and slightly nauseous. The absolute quiet has prompted a ringing in my ears that is getting consistently louder, and the cold has well and truly wrapped its coat around me.

The walls of vapor did not look this thick from the hill. I seem to have been walking for ages. I'm getting worried, considering turning back, but relief kicks in as I finally emerge from the greyness, able to see my limbs once again.

I didn't realize how fast my heart was beating, but as I double over and suck in some of the less icy air, I feel it relentlessly pounding against the wall of my chest.

I made it, though. I'm here.

Like a perfect circle inside, the grass here is so incredibly green and lush, as though the wall around it serves only to preserve its beauty. It is flawless, every blade appears to be the same length, and the color is luxuriantly emerald throughout.

How could there be a rational explanation for this? What bullshit would Dad come up with?

I realize I can no longer see the top edge of the mist, as though the walls have extended towards the sky. Which way was I facing? I grab the compass from my pocket only to find the arrow is stuck, immobile as if there is no magnetic field here. Shit! The flawlessness of mist formation and grass beneath my feet offers no clues at all, and an urgent panic sets in. I need to leave. Which way?

Everywhere I look, I see grey, a cocoon of blandness that no longer offers mystery, just oppressive entrapment. Spurred by the chill that runs through my bones, I turn and begin walking back towards the grey wall, but just as I reach the edge, a deep guttural groan comes from behind that stops me dead in my tracks.

Slowly, I turn to see the ground rising before me like a drawbridge—the groan still emerging, the ground shaking beneath my feet.

My legs won't work. I'm frozen, mesmerized by the opening in the ground that is appearing before me. The earthy trapdoor continues to lift with mechanical precision, a perfect square with approximately eighty-inch sides and a living breathing lid about twenty inches in depth. It spits out more of the grey mist that attaches itself to the existing walls around me. They're closing in on me.

The noise is haunting, as though the earth is letting out a long smoky exhale. A strange noise leaves my lips, a nonsensical garble of disbelief. From the blackness within, I see something spit out from the hole and begin to float towards the floor. I dare not take my eyes away from the moving lid, but from the corner of my eye, I see it land a few feet in front of me. Finally, the groan ends, and the earth stops moving.

Briefly, I move my eyes away towards the crumpled piece of paper on the grass. As I bend down to retrieve it, I notice the unmistakable graphic on the faded wrapper's front.

Jodie's favorite chocolate bar.

Fuck—no!

And I run. I run so fast into the icy cloud around me, each breath so cold and cutting. But the mist doesn't give, and I don't seem to be getting anywhere.

Another groan from behind me.

No—no way!

Urgently, I turn, and the mouth of the earth still looms.

"Steve!" her voice drifts from the blackness.

No, this isn't happening. Please—no!

"Steve, help me, please."

What is this? It can't be real. Is it my imagination—a projection of the guilt that I feel? It must be.

"Steve," her voice again—distant—desolate.

She never took a phone or watch with her that day. My parents blamed me for that, and of course, I blame myself. I went looking for her every day. I thought she would be okay; I thought we would find her. She is strong—was—was so strong. Suddenly, I break down. The tears come, and I begin to bawl uncontrollably.

Her body was never found.

"Please, Steve."

But I can't do it. I can't go in there.

Wiping the damp from my eyes, I slowly start to back away. The word *Sorry* leaves my lips croakily, barely audible.

Something grabs the edge of the grass— not human, but resembling a hand of some sort—brown, twisted and knotted, small spindly branches like fingers. Another earthy hand wraps around the opposite side. More mist expels, and another groan sends tremors towards me.

Holy shit!

As the spindly arms begin to pull the unknown creature from the ground, a pair of bright white eyes emerge from the darkness. I continue my retreat, but I'm not putting any distance between us—it's as though the mist is a gaseous barrier holding me in position. The face finally comes into view with another loud groan, and I let out a silent scream. The makeshift hair is a scattering of dry tinder-like twigs that continues down the muddy cheeks and underneath the chin. Patchy moss decorates the rest of the earthy face, spreading across branches that form the human-like shoulder blades. Even with the foliage covering most of the face and the muddy lichen-ridden complexion, I recognize it to be my sister. Or at least some of her.

The moss that forms the mouth begins to part. "It's so peaceful down here, Steve. But I'm lonely."

As she continues to pull herself from the pit, the first rickety leg plants itself on the grass in front of me. "You'll like it down here, the smells and the gentle patter of rain. We can be part of nature together. For eternity."

I try to speak but can't find any words.

The second leg emerges until it's completely out and thrusting itself to an upright position. It's close enough to touch, standing perhaps seven feet tall in front of me.

I can smell the dampness from the moss that covers her. With each tiny movement, I hear the gentle cracking of the bough that forms her twisted spine.

"J-Jodie."

"It's your fault, Steve. No watch, no phone; that's what you always said. Don't tell anyone where you are going. Otherwise, it's not an adventure anymore."

"But I—"

The right arm reaches towards me and wraps itself around my left ankle.

"I'm sorry, Jodie!" I scream.

The left one follows, stretching itself around my other leg.

"Come on, Brother," she says.

I crouch down and, with both hands, grip the vine-like limbs, trying to work myself free, but they're slippery and strong.

It's useless.

She begins to pull me towards her along the soft wet grass. I can't get any traction.

"Jodie, please!"

I have carried this blame for so long—it's unfair.

I lost her too!

The crippling guilt over the last few months has been unbearable, like a dark cloud that I can't shake. But this is too much. I don't deserve this.

She steps back into the darkness, and I know that this will now be my fate.

"I'm sorry," I plead as the tears stream down both cheeks.

"It's okay. It's nice down here," she says.

And the eyes turn bright red as she slowly sinks into blackness.

I am getting closer to the edge. Soon I'll be in the pit. I claw at the grass, but it does no good—this is how it will end for me. Perhaps this is what I deserve.

The lid begins to come down as I slide towards the hole.

Perhaps Mum and Dad will be pleased to get rid of me. Maybe life will be easier for them—but who will they blame then?

Laughter emerges from the darkness, deep and other-worldly, and I begin to sob with fear. Halfway in, up to my waist. I can see nothing below but the eyes, floating down into the darkness like falling embers. Up to my shoulders now, and the earthy smell of mud fills my nostrils.

This can't be. Jodie didn't have an evil bone in her body.

More laughter.

This thing—it can't be—it's not Jodie.

I grip the edge of the pit with my hands. The lid is almost upon me now, and I'll soon be in complete darkness, underground with whatever that is. I snap my head around to see the last of the mist disappearing and the trees in the distance.

It pulls me inside.

"This wasn't my fault!" I scream as loud as I can. "It wasn't my fucking fault!"

And darkness.

And silence.

I can't breathe. I'm slipping away—dizzy—swimming—the heavy smell of mud—

* * *

I can see my breath. Shaking—freezing—where am I?

The stars. I can see the stars!

Pushing myself up, I look around, trying to get my bearings. I'm back on top of the hill, but there's no longer a ring of mist in the distance, just uneven, brown ground and a scattering of trees swaying in the evening breeze.

What the hell just happened? Did I fall asleep? Was that a—dream? I need to get out of here. How long have I been asleep?

As I fumble through my pocket, my fingers finally lock around the compass, and urgently, I yank it out, sending the scrunched-up wrapper flying into the air. It falls to the ground, landing next to my right foot. For a fleeting moment, I think I hear a distant groan but figure it might be the wind blowing through the trees. I stare at the wrapper, thinking about picking it up, but—she's gone.

She's gone.

I don't think we will ever find out what happened to her. She belongs to the earth now—damp and rotten—overwhelmed by the darkness. Whatever I experienced was preying on my guilt, trying to lure me in, and it nearly got me.

But I won't carry the blame anymore. I won't!

I don't think I'll be hiking around here for a while. It's time to let go, find a different spot. This land feels bad now.

I need to get home. Mum and Dad will be worried. Hopefully.

Ant Lion

Matthew Hughes

"Why do you watch this crap?" she said from the doorway. "Those people are nothing but vultures, picking some poor soul's bones."

"Actually, I was thinking about that," he said. "These abandoned lockers they bid on, they're some guy's entire worldly goods."

"Exactly," she said, "and a bunch of loud-mouth scavengers–"

"But how does that happen? I mean, they find antiques, coin collections, designer clothing–who walks away from all that?"

She shrugged. "Thousands of people disappear every year and are never heard from again."

"Sure, yeah, runaway kids get picked up by paedophiles, crazies throw themselves into rivers and get washed out to sea. But look at that."

On the screen, a pot-bellied man with a goatee was holding up a framed Picasso and declaring that this was why he was the king.

He turned to her. "Somebody owns a Picasso, and he just walks off into the sunset?"

"I don't care," she said. "Turn it off."

He changed the channel. Next up was Morgan Freeman, talking about how there could be other dimensions that we're not equipped to see, the way water-striding insects can't imagine the dangerous depths beneath them.

"Oh, what does he know?" she said. "He's just an actor."

He changed the channel again. Up came a nature documentary. She moved into the room and sat down. She liked wildlife, even bugs.

The screen showed an ant in a conical-shaped depression of sand so finely grained that the insect couldn't climb out. Its struggles only served to make it slide down to the bottom of the pit—where something waited, buried.

A man with glasses and a bowtie was saying how ants probably wouldn't ever believe in ant lions, "Because no ant ever met one and came back to tell the tale."

On the screen, the ant was being pulled under the surface by something that couldn't be clearly seen. After a moment, the sand was clear, pristine.

"Yuck," he said. "I'm going down to the corner, get some beers."

Her eyes were on the screen. "Get me some gum."

* * *

The street was empty but full of afternoon sun. He wished he'd worn sunglasses. He crossed over and went past the little park. Something flashed and flickered in the corner of his vision, under one of the big evergreens, like a fine, jeweled thread vertically spinning. He went to take a closer look.

It was in the shade, close to the trunk, shining. He ducked under the lowest branches, got closer, but still couldn't make it out.

Then he realized it was suddenly much darker than it should have been. He turned to look back the way he had come but saw nothing but blackness in all directions.

That's weird, he thought. *Eclipse?*

He had straightened up. Where were the branches? Where was the tree? He put out his arms, felt nothing.

"What the heck is—" he said. But then he definitely felt something. And it definitely felt him.

He didn't even have time to appreciate the irony.

The Divergence in the Woods

Dawn Vogel

Somewhere in the dark forest is where we lost track of Dad. One minute, he was there, and the next, he was gone.

Our stepmom didn't seem surprised when we came back without him. "The dark forest gives, and the dark forest takes."

Lara and I didn't accept that. So we went back to look for him.

The problem was we didn't know exactly where we'd lost him, and the dark forest is a big place.

It's been ten years. Our stepmom is gone now. And Lara and I agreed that we're not going to stop looking until we find him.

Lara borrowed a micrometer accuracy GPS device from the university where she's a grad student. She says I don't want to know how much it cost.

I've been saving up my money for mountain climbing equipment. There aren't any mountains to climb, but we're going to be tethered together with straps that can withstand a serious drop. The dark forest won't take us.

Neither of us wants to consider what it means if we cover every inch of the dark forest and don't find him.

We've gridded out the entirety of the forest. We've eliminated the edges—if he'd been lost there, we'd have found him as teens. But we check there anyway, just in case.

Could he still be in the forest, alive? Or are we looking for a skeleton?

Lara's frowning at the GPS device, rotating to sweep the signal across a chunk of the woods, somewhere in the middle of grid D-12. Her waterproof jacket and pants brush against each other as she turns, producing a faint whispery sound.

I can almost believe it's Dad calling us from just beyond the edge of hearing.

"There's an anomaly." She's turned on her LED headlamp and the halogen lantern, shining them both into the distance.

The darkness swallows the light like it's just a pair of nightlight bulbs, not serious wattage.

We look at each other.

"Where is it on the map?" I ask.

We take a moment to spread out the map, find our location, and circle the portion of the grid we're in. We both snap a photo of the darkness and the map with our cellphones, even though neither of us has a signal, and we can't send them to anyone.

"We should check the rest, for other anomalies," I suggest.

Lara nods. "Let's flag this one first."

We stake out the edge of the area with neon orange flags, giving the anomaly itself a wide berth. When we're done, it's a rough circle of fluttering brightness surrounding the dark spot in the center. It doesn't seem like enough to contain it, but at least it might keep someone else from wandering into the area.

After the anomaly, the rest of the dark forest seems bright and cheery, with nothing else that gives Lara pause. Except for the utter stillness of it all. We've had to push that out of our minds.

There's nowhere else that Dad could be.

We know where to go.

In spite of the tether between us, we take each other's hand, like we did when we were kids, facing the anomaly.

"Ready?" Lara asks.

"No. Are you?"

"No."

I glance at her. "We gonna do this anyway?"

"I am if you are."

Just like when we were kids, always trying to keep up with each other, to outperform, to be noticed and praised. Maybe that's why we're both so dead set on finding Dad.

I pull my phone out of my pocket, wedge it into a crook in a nearby tree.

"What are you doing?" Lara asks.

I shrug. "Maybe there's a signal in there, and we can ping my phone from yours. Maybe my phone will be the only thing that gets us out." I don't say what I'm really thinking.

Maybe my phone will be the only proof that we were here.

Lara shakes her head, but she doesn't try to dissuade me from leaving my phone behind. I think she knows what I'm thinking too.

We take each other's hand again, holding tightly.

We're going to find him.

We're going into the anomaly, and we might not be coming back.

The dark forest gives, and the dark forest takes.

Living with Dying

Kevin Brown

Blotting my lips with my napkin, I slide my plate away and look across the table at Helen. She's thousand-yard-staring at her untouched dinner. It's her favorite—homemade meatloaf and sweet potatoes, with a slice of Mandarin Orange cake. I've made it for her every evening since we got the news. I hoped it would cheer her up. Remind her life is full of simple pleasures. But she won't touch it. I've even had to spoon-feed her on several occasions, as if she's a child. As if she's the one who's dying.

I close my eyes and take a few deep breaths. The frustration of it all, dealing with her dealing with me. When I open them, for a second, I see the vibrant woman I've loved for forty-five years. I see her hollow eyes catch light and her slack expression stretch into that room-stopping smile. My wife. My life. I can't and never could stay angry with her.

I brush a mouse-tail of gray hair from her forehead, place my hand on hers, and say, "You have to eat, hon."

No answer.

"No need in both of us getting sick."

Silence.

A fly lands on the rim of her plate and scuttles around. I swat it away, take the dishes to the sink. Gathering the nerve, I throw my head back and finish my glass of wine. Immediately, it doubles me over, a starburst of needles in the cavity walls of my stomach. I imagine it, black and rotten and pocked along my guts like mold. A living, growing monster, eating away at the core. Swallowing me, inside out, from the world. Though the pain is so intense it takes my breath away, I drink the wine because I like to think it pisses it off in there. Just a little.

After a minute, it passes and I'm able to breathe again. "Take that you son of a bitch," I whisper.

My wife hasn't moved and that hurts worse than the filth inside. I saw the first part of her fade the day of my diagnosis. The day I found out something was eating me, something else began eating her. That day, I stepped into the lobby where she was waiting and said, "Helen? Could you come here a second?"

She followed me to the examination room, a strained smile on her face. Her eyes never leaving me.

"Leighton?" she said.

"Sit down," I said, feeling like a tree branch was being shaken inside my body from what the doctor had just told me. From what he was about to tell her. When I nodded and tried to give her a smile, I could tell that without knowing, she knew.

I walk behind her at the table, rub her shoulders. I kiss the side of her head and say, "Wanna sit by your garden?"

I get her up and out to her garden in the back yard. To her white wicker chair where she liked to sit, admiring her work after tending its rows-on-rows of lilies and tulips. Sunflowers and geraniums. Before my check-up, she'd begun to plant tomatoes and cucumbers, and had her sights set on eggplants and corn.

After that day though, her garden began to flood with weeds. The plants browning, a scatter-shot of holes in their leaves. The flowers bowed and wilted as quickly as she did. So now, I keep it up. I had to look online to learn how to plant, what top-soils and manure to use, how much and how often to water. Every day, I'm on my knees, biting down so hard at the pain that my gums hurt, weeding and manicuring so each night after dinner she'll have something thriving and beautiful and full of life to look at.

I can't say it's working, and I've got six months or less to find something that does.

I go back inside and do the dishes. I watch her through the window over the kitchen sink. So many evenings I've watched her through this very window, spraying down her "babies." And they were her babies because we were never able to have children. The day we found out, we sat in a doctor's office, hearing news that would change our lives. The same way we would hear life-changing news years later. A single tear slid off her cheek. Then, she smiled, laid her head against my chest, and said, "It's okay. We've got each other."

And we did. And I've watched her through this window, young and strong, catching fireflies and smiling at them glowing in her cupped hand, the town spread out beyond her. Watched her brown hair become streaked with gray then turn completely white, the outline of the town changing with her. We've had careers, traveled. We've grown old together the way we planned. But now I'm leaving her. We knew we'd die someday. We're all living with dying around us, coming toward us. But it's different when it's on the horizon, flat-lining like an evening sun in the distance.

At first, she blamed God, but there's no way to release rage against God. So she blamed me. Told me I was abandoning her. Screamed and yelled until the screams and yells became less frequent, then stopped altogether.

The last thing she said was, "You lied. You said you'd never leave me."

Then silence. She began her descent into catatonia. Allowed her own monster to eat away at her core, swallow her inside out from the world. And if I can't shake her out of it, they'll put her into a home. That isn't the last image I want before I go. I want her out in the yard, hose in hand, with her babies.

When it begins to get dark, I go out and get her. Fireflies dot the sky and I catch one, put it in her palm, and watch it light her hand, then lift away.

Inside, I run her a bath and ease her into the tub. Leaning over the side, the monster is chewing. I sponge her back and arms and cup handfuls of water over her hair. I towel her off and slip her nightgown on. Get her into bed. Watching her while she sleeps, I try to take in every image of her. To fill me with enough to get by on the other side, if there is one. The funny thing is, it's only her I'm afraid for. How would I deal with losing her? You can mourn, deal with it, move forward. You can give up and slip into somewhere else, finding more fear in an unknown tomorrow than the dead certainty of how tomorrow ends.

"Don't give up," I say, aloud. She doesn't stir.

I switch off the bedside lamp and drape my arm over her the way I have done since the beginning. Tomorrow, I will try harder. My wife. My life. With one, the other will not fade. Before I go, I will bring her back.

I'm leaving, I tell her with my mind, hoping she somehow hears me somewhere else. *But don't leave me, Helen. Keep me alive inside you the way you did your lilies and geraniums, your roses and forget-me-nots. Your babies. Don't give up on the morning. I am here with you tonight.*

I will sleep as I have slept for forty-five years, with my arm draped over Helen. I will snuggle tight to what she used to be. I'll caress a body whose only light is the moon glow off her decaying remains. And I will sleep tonight and awaken beside her in the morning to another day lonely, but not alone.

The Lonely Grave

Leonora Lewis

"Did the rain bomb catch her on the Long Bridge?"

Marigold Satterwhite knew her daughter-in-law was dead before the two Louisiana State Troopers standing on her front porch said anything. She and Nathan had heard the old Seth Thomas clock— the clock that ticked down all the births and deaths in her family—chime once at 5:20 pm yesterday during the worst of the storm.

The troopers twist their hats in their hands. They're shocked at how callous she sounds, but Marigold will be damned if she's going to cry in front of them. Her great-grandmother Paxton told her, "Never say die! Say damn!"

Before Marigold can ask them if the cat's got their tongues, the big one with the mustache remembers their script, "Ma'am, we're sorry to inform you of Alexandra Satterwhite's death. Her car got swept away in the flood waters."

"She's drowned. As drowned as Denham Springs." Marigold puts her hand over her heart thinking about that bridge crossing miles and miles of water—covering what used to be Denham Springs. "Not coming from here, she didn't know it's a bad place to get trapped."

Marigold had put Nathan on the phone to talk with Alex.

"Find a motel. You can't outdrive that supercell. It's going to explode and dump enough water on you to fill the Mississippi River," Nathan told her before the call dropped.

"Alexandra was coming to Baton Rouge to be closer to us," Marigold tells the troopers. Even before a distraught Alex called, Marigold had thought about hearing the clock chime for Jeff six months ago . "Nathan and I are all she had left besides the baby she was expecting. Her Hmong kin had nothing to do with her because her father was African American."

Nathan comes up behind Marigold, "St. Paul's Symphony's second violin section's loss."

"Dr. Satterwhite." Both officers stop short of saluting.

Marigold sees a Louisiana Swamp Cat venture out of the woods onto the lawn behind the troopers. She's never seen one come out in the open in the middle of the day. The cats prefer the woods where their gray fur with swirling black bulls-eye stripes mixes with dappled light and shadows.

"Which one?" Nathan asks them, "My wife has a Ph.D. in Medieval History."

Marigold sees Nathan take in the Swamp Cat's presence, but he doesn't do anything to call the troopers' attention to it.

Behind the men, the cat stands up on its back legs and walks a few steps leaning forward, the way Swamp Cats do, bristling its whiskers, ears forward and brow scrunched up over its green eyes.

"About that," the big officer clears his throat while the other one keeps eyeing the trees surrounding our property. "Someone got the deceased out of the car and did a crude C-section. They left her there with flowers and leaves scattered over her. We put out a bulletin to look out for anyone turning in a preemie."

Marigold feels her heart slam hard in her chest. The clock chimed once. It only chimed for Alex.

The cat puts its clever front paws together—the ones it uses to get into garbage cans—and started rocking side to side, while focusing its gaze on Nathan. It hooks its extra, sixth toes and flutters its digits like it's making a bird shadow puppet at Nathan before dropping down on all fours and bounding off, the officers none the wiser.

"You think whoever took the baby went into the swamp." Nathan says.

"Yes, Sir, I do," The big officer replies.

When the officers leave, Nathan gets up, puts on his battered old hat to keep the sun and rain off his head; his once wavy red-brown hair is now salted with gray. "I'm going into the swamps to find our grandchild."

* * *

Marigold watches Nathan circling the site where the Amite River had laid Alex to rest. She tries not to think about the officers finding Alex: her blue almond-shaped eyes, that always stood out against her terracotta complexion, closed as if in sleep; her long dark hair spread out; her blood soaking into the ground.

Love had brought Alex on that final trip to Baton Rouge.

Love had led Marigold to Nathan. She, a professor of medieval history at LSU, never expected to find love in her late thirties with a forestry/botany grad student, ten years younger, from Mississippi. She knew from the first that she'd have to share him with his other loves: the forests, swamps, and trees.

"Here," Nathan kneels, pointing out the tracks left in the muddy bank. "The highway patrol did their best. They didn't know what to look for."

Looking over his shoulder, Marigold sees the faint impressions of four long toes, three facing forward, one back.

"Stornes!" The thought of those large birds with their teeth and claws circling Alex's body sends a jolt of pain against Marigold's sternum. They didn't eat Alex; they took the baby... She didn't want to go there.

Nathan walks back to the spot while studying the grasses. Then he heads towards the edge of the woods, stopping to bend down, grasp a bent weed stalk and scrutinize it. He stands up facing the forest.

He'd gone into the woods and dealt with Stornes before, and walked away alive. Marigold thought about all those times that she waited at home praying not to hear that old Seth Thomas clock chime for him.

She feels a couple more pains in her chest. "Those waders you bought me for our anniversary are in the trunk. The trees will tolerate me if I'm with you."

Nathan stopped, "This isn't like the times you helped me collect specimens."

On their first date, Marigold had helped Nathan look for leeches for a colleague of his. A few years later she held up their toddler son to say "Hi" to that same colleague's favorite slime mold.

From the way Nathan's looking at her, he knows she's having chest pains. "I took my heart medication this morning," she added.

Everything goes silent when Marigold steps into the trees. No more bird or insect song. Nathan goes ahead to push the branches out of the way, keeping hold of them so they don't whip back in her face. He tramps hard enough to give warning to any snakes slithering around.

The canopy looms over Marigold and she feels the trees' presence. They're aware of her, but she's with Nathan. The trees accept Nathan, a man whose ancestors learned to walk the woods with the Choctaw.

She follows him, making sure to keep her footing on the banks of the creek that feeds into the Amite. The water's still high with a fast-moving current.

Rustling in the brush startles her. A swamp cat bursts out of the undergrowth in front of her. It rises onto its back legs, eyes wide and startled, and hisses before plunging back into the undergrowth. Marigold stifles a laugh.

The overhead sun turns the leaves and branches into black and white silhouettes. They move by themselves in the still air, forming patterns. They're starting to look like the faces in all those black and white family photos that her mother passed on to her.

Photos of Marigold's great-grandmother Paxton and her sisters and parents, the Birds, spread out on the table. Older tintypes show the Stanebridges: including Thaddeus Stanebridge in his Union uniform.

Marigold hears her long-dead mother's voice whispering in the wind blowing through the leaves. "Don't marry him."

The trees are releasing chemicals. They're affecting her mind.

The light and shadows morph into a face. The face in that picture Marigold's mother had shown her once: Eliezer, Thaddeus's half-brother, who was a lifelong bachelor and the family recluse. Even in black and white, Marigold makes out his split upper lip, his cat-like profile.

She realizes she's standing there, hand over her heart.

Nathan's looking at her, concerned, "You're seeing things."

"I know what I'm seeing is not real," she said.

Nathan starts to say something. Instead, he stands there listening.

Marigold hears a baby crying far away.

"Dragon Fighter."

Marigold starts at the sound of that raspy voice.

There's a Storne standing in the shadow of a sweet bay tree on its long wading bird legs. A six-footer.

Nathan walks up to the Storne like it's the most natural thing in the world. The Storne bobs its head on its long neck, tucking it into an S curve, then straightening it out again. Marigold sees the flash of three digits with claws extending beyond its wing tips and stands still.

People mistake Stornes for herons, egrets and cranes. Stornes don't let most people get close enough to spot the differences. Those that do don't live to regret it.

Marigold follows after Nathan making sure not to make any sudden movements. Nathan knows what he's doing. The Stornes remember Nathan. Ten years ago, he tracked and killed a giant man-eating snake in Florida; it had crashed the ecosystem consuming almost all living animals. He'd called the devastation a dragon waste. Nathan helped the Storne survivors from that flock join their Louisiana cousins.

The Storne bows its head to Nathan, gives its body a shake and fluffs up, then relaxes, its feathers.

"You have our grandchild," Nathan says.

"*Oui.* We find your kin *morte*, but *la bébé, elle n'est pas morte.*

We bring *bébé* out into world. You gave us our *famille*, we give *votre famille.*"

Looking over Nathan's shoulder, Marigold sees the teeth in the Storne's beak.

"Avec moi."

It turns and strides along the ground, keeping its sickle toe claw out of the mud. The jungle and vines and the creek open up to a small lake created by the flooding. The crying has stopped. Marigold hears gurgling. The sounds a happy baby makes.

On a small island of high ground, Stornes roosting on low hanging branches are screeching, "Traack! Traack!" and flapping their wings in agitation, while others fly out skimming low over the water.

Their Storne guide starts jumping up and down, hopping mad. "*La bébé! Les Chats!* "

Marigold sees three Louisiana swamp cats, using a Storne nest as a pirogue, poling away from the island.

Their Storne launches into the air to join others dive-bombing the Swamp Cats. The cats strike at the Storne with the sticks they're using as poles.

"Hey there!" Nathan is wading out into the water. Marigold watches him, trying not to think about water moccasins and gators. Her heavy waders keep her from floundering in after him. Nathan doesn't need to end up rescuing her if she steps off into a deep place.

Two cats go over the side of their makeshift boat and start swimming —pushing the boat before them. The Stornes keep attacking the cat still in the boat. It hisses and ducks.

"Stop it!" Nathan roars at the Stornes.

The Stornes stop their attack. Water up over his knees, Nathan catches up to the floating nest and catches hold of it.

"Cats, you know that baby doesn't belong here. It doesn't belong with you either."

The two cats in the water and the one in the boat cock their heads like they're listening. Then the swamp cat in the nest goes over the side and all three swim off.

The Storne lands on the rim of the nest. Flapping its wings, it propels the nest to shore, Nathan alongside, before flying off to rejoin its flock on the little island.

Nathan picks up the squirming infant, wrapped in fairly clean rags, "The Stornes or the cats must have cleaned her up."

Marigold holds out her arms for the child.

Nathan hesitates a second before handing over the baby, "I remember how quiet your mother got when I mentioned that before the revolution the Stanebridges intermarried with the Satterwhites. Neither of us would have done differently."

Marigold looks down at her granddaughter who is waving her small fists with a smile on her adorable, cat-like face.

"The past can't be changed," she reassures him. "The *now* affects the future. I love her now."

A river birch spins up to her. Until the trees saved the world, no one knew trees could move like that: spinning in the direction they want to go, covering up their tracks behind them.

Now, instead of a river birch, her great-grandmother Paxton—tall and unbent even at a hundred, when Marigold last saw her—stands there.

Marigold clutches her granddaughter to her chest, "I know this isn't real. You're using your defenses to make me see you like this. "

Nathan lays a reassuring hand on her shoulder "They're communicating. It's not an attack."

"I'm pleased you didn't let your mother scare you. Most things that frighten you don't happen or don't happen the way you think they will." The image of great-grandmother Paxton beams at Marigold before fading away, leaving Marigold facing a river birch.

Bloody Sunday

Victory Witherkeigh

"This camp isn't like the others," our dad said when he first told us to pack our backpacks. "It's being run by our college alma mater."

"Yep," Mom chimed in. "That's where we met, ya know? They put us on the same dorm floor first year."

My brother and I cut her off, rolling our eyes at the thought of hearing about how they met. "We know the story, Mom. You tell us all the time."

"Anyway," she said, wagging her finger at my face, "this camp trip is for all of us. There are activities meant for just you two now that you're in middle school. You'll love it: hiking, crafts, and songs! And then we'll have shows and skits the counselors put on for us. There's disco bingo, a pool party..."

She went on and on forever.

The campgrounds were in the Sierra mountains near Yosemite national park. But the thing my brother and I got the biggest kick out of was our counselors. They were all college kids, a majority who attended the University of California school system like my parents. They may have thought we were too young to notice the scent of the beer on their breaths when the lifeguard called us for pool time or to see them walk to the back of the craft shed after tie-dying our shirts, coughing up thick white smoke with bloodshot eyes. They were a mixture of girls and boys, but they always seemed to talk about the same things when they thought the campers weren't listening: the Saturday night parties and the Lady of the Gulch.

"Do you have your costume ready for the big 'M' on Saturday?" The lead hiking guide mumbled, rubbing his temples.

The other counselor shrugged before saying, "Eh, it's basically done. As long as I can avoid the 'Lady of the Gulch,' I'm fine..."

We asked our parents when we got back to our half cabin, half tent, if they had ever heard of the "Lady of the Gulch."

"Oh, yeah," our father shook his head as he spoke, "children can't wander in the gulch alone, or the Lady will come and take you away..."

"*What?*" My brother and I looked at one another, eyes bulging, jaws dropped before turning back to him, "Why would she take kids?"

"It's an unfortunate story," he said, fluffing his sleeping bag to brush off any extra dirt. "When the camp first opened, back in the late 1940s, a new widow came with her child, hoping the campgrounds would help lift their spirits after her husband passed away. The camp back then only had the Gold campsite, and her young child ended up lost during one hike. It was said the woman went mad, refusing to leave the area, wandering the woods in search of her kid. When she couldn't find him, she killed herself, haunting the gulch to take in any strays."

"No way, Dad," I said with a scowl. "Stop making stuff up."

"I'm not," he said. "It's the reason we've always walked with you between the campgrounds of Gold and Blue."

I rolled my eyes at him before looking over at my brother. I knew as I looked into my brother's dark brown eyes that we would find the 'M' party the counselors talked about. We waited for the tell-tale snores of our dad to begin before grabbing the small flashlights to head up the dark trail.

"C'mon, hurry!" my older brother said, hissing at me as we scoured up the dirt hill.

"Shh! Keep your voice down," I replied, eyes bulging back at him as I scoffed. "The point was to sneak up on them, not get caught, idiot..."

He rolled his eyes back at me before continuing up the dirt pathway cut between the lush forest and large craggy rocks towards the camp's main wellness center. The glow of soft strobe lights flicked through the dark woods as the thrum of a deep bass beat vibrated under our sneakers.

"I think we're close..."

Crunch.

"Hahhahahhaha,"

A crackling, hysterical laugh whistled through the dark woods around us.

"Did you hear that?" my brother said, his voice rising an octave. "Someone is coming!"

We spun around, scrambling down the dirt path as quickly as possible. The pounding of my converse sneakers against the dirt and mangled tree roots echoed with my brother's own stomping as the dust kicked up behind us. Trees and rocks blurred as we ran as fast as we could down the hill, into the gulch between Gold and Blue, towards our cabin.

"What the—"

My brother stopped in front of me just before the stream separating the two campgrounds. I was running so fast, I couldn't stop myself from running into him, sending us both crashing to the ground.

"Ugh... What was th—"

I never finished my sentence. As I rolled over to my knees, a woman stood in the middle of the creek, her skin a slimy, pale green peeking from her tattered long dress. Her long, black hair hung across one eye, covered with the same green moss and foliage that the forest floor showed us on our morning walks.

She stared directly at my brother and me before her jaw lowered to a hair-raising guttural moan as the slash across her throat opened with her cries.

Dark, thick drops of green sludge splattered across my face, the smell of putrid wet mud and thick earthy moss stifling against the back of my throat. Choking and coughing against the taste of rotting wood and ash as the moonlight glow crept over the treetops, the light faded slowly as she dragged us down into the mud.

"It's okay, baby," she croaked. "Mommy's here . . ."

Red Oak's Revenge

James Blakey

The oldest tree in the North Woods is Red Oak. The memories of a thousand cycles of sun and snow live in its trunk, branches, leaves, roots. Its sap flows with the stories of jack pines, white birches, sugar maples, choke cherries, and millions of their cousins who cover the Porcupine Mountains.

* * *

The eight-speaker stereo system thumps with Kid Rock's raspy voice.

"Maybe you should slow down." Wendy clutches the grab handle. Her left hand braces against the glove compartment.

Robby bounces in his seat. "Hold on!" The black F-150 blasts through a puddle as wide as the logging road. Mud-colored water splashes the windshield. "That was the best one yet."

Wendy presses her hiking boots against the floorboard, her neck against the headrest in a vain attempt to stop her teeth from rattling.

"Here's the turn-off." Robby downshifts to second. The transmission whines like a baby missing his bottle. The truck powers up the incline.

The road, more a glorified hiking trail, isn't much wider than the truck. Branches scrape the sides, scratch the paint.

"Watch out!" Wendy yells.

Robbie slams the brakes. A twelve-point buck dashes in front of the truck, then disappears into the woods.

Robbie shakes his head at the missed opportunity. "Should've brought my rifle. My grandma has the best recipe for venison stew."

Wendy utters a silent prayer that they make it to the campsite in one piece.

Ten minutes of lurching ascent brings them to a clearing. Robby kills the engine. Hints of sunlight, blue sky filter through the thick mass of red and yellow leaves.

Wendy steps down from the cab, inhales the pine-scented air, warm for early October. "This is amazing, almost worth the ride." She tosses Robby her phone. "Snap a photo of me." Wendy shakes out her red hair, poses with a foot raised on a downed tree, flashes a smile of dazzling white teeth.

Robby obliges, taking half a dozen shots.

Wendy scrolls through the images, selects the cutest one, and uploa . . .— "Damn. No bars."

"Up here, we're getting away from everything. Including Instagram." Robbie snatches the phone, blue eyes twinkling, stuffs it in his jacket pocket.

"Give it back." Wendy reaches for the phone.

"Nope." Robby smiles, chin dimpling, and twists out of her grasp.

Wendy curls her hands into fists, faux hits Robby in the chest. He grabs her wrists. She loses her balance. Robby tries to prevent her fall. Now he's the one tumbling to the ground, landing in a pile of leaves, Wendy on top of him. Laughter turns to kisses.

* * *

After each snow cycle, new saplings burst through the forest floor, stretching for the sky, reaching for the light and warmth of the sun.

The younglings listen in silent horror as Red Oak tells tales of lightning strikes sparking ravaging infernos and bark-burrowing beetles eating their kin from inside out.

But the scariest stories Red Oak knows are those of the humans.

Humans with their mighty saws who slaughter entire hillsides, hauling away trunks to be carved up in their mills.

Humans who bring forth blights that killed the chestnuts and Dutch elms.

Humans flying overhead in noisy metal tubes, destroying the tranquility of the forest, disrupting nature's balance, slowly boiling the Earth.

* * *

"Check this out." Wendy points at the trunk of a butternut hickory.

Robby squints. "What about it?"

"The pattern on the bark. It looks like the face of an old witch watching us. An angry witch." Wendy traces the outline. "See? Here's her frown. And this is her pointed hat."

"I'm not a fan of voyeurs." Robby pulls the knife from his belt, chips away the bark, destroying the face. He carves a heart into the exposed phloem. Wendy uses her knife to scratch out their initials. Robby gives her back the phone; the couple poses for a photo around their handiwork.

"We need to set up camp." Robbie heads back to the truck, grabs the rolled-up tent from the bed. "Why don't you collect some firewood? Look for dead dry branches. Not too thick."

Wendy rolls her eyes. "I know the difference between good and bad firewood." She wanders off, leaves crunching under her boots. A few hundred feet later, she stops. Pinpricks teased the back of her neck. A sensation that someone is watching her, staring at her. Like high school, when creepy old men would turn out to watch her play volleyball.

Wendy stands still. The silence of the forest is interrupted by the occasional high-pitched *churry, churry, churry, chorry, chorry* of a mourning warbler. She shakes off the feeling, focuses on her task, gathers the kindling. But the pinpricks return, more intense. She spins like a ballroom dancer, certain she's going to catch whomever is watching. Spotting a badger, a fox, even a squirrel staring at her would be a relief. But Wendy sees only trees.

* * *

The saplings rustle their leaves, demanding action, justice, for the cruelty, humiliation inflicted upon their cousin. Red Oak hears their lamentations, understands their anger. For too long the humans have used the forest for their personal amusement.

* * *

Wendy holds two camping forks over the fire. One has her hot dog, the other is skewered with half-a-dozen marshmallows. "I can't shake the feeling that someone is watching me."

"Someone is." Robby sips his Bell's.

"Huh?" Wendy twists her neck, nothing but flickering shadows.

"It's me. I'm watching the hottest girl in the U.P."

Wendy blushes, tosses a marshmallow at Robby.

He snatches it, popping it in his mouth, chugs the rest of the bottle. "Want another?"

Wendy nods. "And pass the mustard."

Robby retrieves two bottles from the cooler. Wendy cradles the hotdog with a bun, slides it off the fork, adds mustard and relish.

She was skeptical when Robby suggested a weekend in the woods. But the food's hot, and the drinks are cold. In the light of the fire, Robby fills out his flannel shirt nicely. With each bottle, the boy is looking cuter and cuter.

* * *

Beneath the forest floor an interdependent network of roots links the brotherhood of trees, carrying Red Oak's call to action. Soon the entirety of the North Woods knows what must be done.

* * *

Inside the tent Wendy shivers in her t-shirt. She flips over her pillow, then presses against Robby in their double sleeping bag, trying to steal his body heat. She checks her watch: 2:34. When is she going to fall asleep?

Crack!

Wendy holds her breath, waiting, listening.

Thirty seconds of silence is broken by hooting. Is that a Barred Owl or a Barn Owl? Wendy's mom would know.

Crack!

"Wake up!" She shakes Robbie's shoulders.

"Huh? I thought you were tired out. But you want more?" Robby reaches for her.

"No." Wendy slaps his hand away. "I heard a noise. Like something's moving around out there."

"I don't he . . ."

"Shush." Wendy crawls out of the sleeping bag, fumbles in the darkness, locates the flashlight, flicks it on. Teeth chattering. She grabs her U of M sweatshirt and convertible pants, slips them on. Wendy zips open the tent, pokes her head out.

"Come back." Robby grabs her foot.

"Stop!" Wendy shakes free. She's outside, standing, spinning the beam three hundred sixty degrees. No bears or bobcats.

Crack!

"Huh?" It's coming from above. Wendy squints, aims the beam skyward.

Nothing but trees.

A great thump in front of her. Robby cries out in pain. She illuminates the tent. It's collapsed under a giant branch.

"Robby!" Wendy rushes to the tent, claws her way through the opening, finds Robby buried in blue plastic, writhing in pain. "Are you okay?"

Robby's groaning, panting. Blood trickles from tiny scratches on his face.

She aims the beam at his body. A piece of the branch that pierced the tent is lodged in his left arm. "Not good, Robby."

"Can you help me yank it out?"

"Uh, uh." She shakes her head. "It might have punctured your brachial artery. Remove it, you could bleed out. What I can do is cut away the rest, so we can get you out of this tent.

Robby grunts his approval. "There's a handsaw in the Ford."

Wendy races to the truck, searches for the saw, feels the pinpricks again. Can't be bothered with that now. She grabs the tool, races back to Robby.

Robby grits his teeth, while Wendy hacks away, tossing aside pieces of branch. When she's done, there's a six-inch spike jutting out of his arm.

"Come outside, so I can get a better look at your arm."

Robbie hobbles out on his knees.

Wendy slices away his torn shirt sleeve. "We need to get you to the hospital. Try to keep the branch from moving."

He sighs. "Driving on these logging roads at night is pretty dangerous. Let's wait for sunrise."

"Robby, as a medical professional, I'm telling you we need to go. Now! It's going to take us a couple of hours to get the hospital in Ontonagon. Things could get much worse in the meantime."

"A year studying nursing at Bay de Noc makes you a professional?"

"That's a year more than you." Wendy softens her voice, puts a hand on his good shoulder. "Robby, I'm serious."

Robby yawns. "All I want to do is go back to sleep."

"Which sounds like you're losing blood, maybe internally. You should be wired, hopped up on adrenaline."

"Okay, let's go." Robby tries to stand.

"Lean on me." Wendy leads Robby to the truck, helps him into the passenger seat. She climbs in the other side.

"What about my gear?" Robby asks.

"Leave it." Wendy checks her phone, still no bars.

"What if someone swipes it? It's brand new. Cost me close to six hundred."

"Guys!" Wendy shakes her head. "You might lose a limb or your life, but God forbid someone takes your stuff. I'll come back to pick it up after I get you to the hospital," she lies.

* * *

Frustrated saplings shake their leaves, twist their branches. The humans must not escape.

Red Oak concurs, but a sacrifice is required. Red Oak offers a way to make death meaningful, become a hero in a story to be told for ten thousand cycles of sun and snow.

The wind carries his request, returns an answer from a Norway maple. Few leaves, peeling bark, rotting roots. One more storm, one more hard freeze, that will be the end. The Norway maple welcomes the peace of death, agrees to what is asked.

***

"How you doing?" Wendy squeezes Robby's hand. Cold. Clammy.

He squeezes back. "Hanging in there. I think you're right about the hospital."

"If nothing else, this trip got you to admit I'm right about something."

Robby laughs, degenerating into a coughing fit.

They're doing barely ten miles per hour. Wendy keeps her foot off the brake, the transmission regulating their descent. The truck staggers from pothole to pothole, comes to a 't' in the road.

Wendy looks left, right. "I'm going to need some help getting out of here. It all looks the same in the dark."

Robby squints at the road. "Go left."

Wendy turns, powers through puddles, builds up enough speed to shift into second.

"Three or four miles and we turn left again," Robby says. "There will be an ol—"

The windshield shatters. The truck slams to a stop. The engine stalls.

"Wh—what happened?" A disoriented Wendy pushes away the deflating airbag.

"Tree." Robby wasn't wearing his seatbelt. His head slammed against the windshield. More blood dribbles down his face.

Wendy eases out of the truck, her knee jammed in the crash. The trunk laying on the hood must be two feet thick. She vainly tries to push the tree off the truck, doesn't budge.

Maybe she can back up. Wendy climbs into the truck. The engine won't turn over. She slams the steering wheel. "What else can go wrong?"

"Wendy, I think my leg is broke." Robbie's voice is distant, like it's coming from the bottom of a pit.

Wendy fights back tears. "Are you sure?"

Robby coughs. "Oh, it's busted. But it feels weird, like it's bloating up." His eyes close, head slumps to the side.

"Robby!" Wendy shakes him, he doesn't answer. She's got to calm down, on the verge of hyperventilating. No time to panic. Closes her eyes, counts backward from ten, comes up with a plan. She'll walk, even on this damn knee, till she finds help or gets cell service.

Back out of the truck. Wendy scrambles over the trunk, the toe of her boot catches on something. Sprawls forward, falling on the point of a broken branch, slides between two ribs.

She's wheezing, stuck on the branch. Can't lift herself up. Is this what a punctured lung feels like? She reaches for the phone. Bars now? Really?

Wendy gulps air, her hand shakes. Tries to call 9-1-1, fingers twitch. Phone slips from her hand. Can't reach it. Leans forwar— "Argh!" The branch slices deeper. Can't catch her breath. Colder. Number. Wendy's eyes close for the last time.

On the ground the phone displays the image of the smiling couple around the carved heart.

* * *

Each spring, on the night of the first full moon after the leaves return, birds stop singing and insects cease buzzing. The whole of the North Woods waits in silence for Red Oak to tell the story of the two humans who carved their mark into a tree and how the forest fought back.

Ties of Love

Lawrence Schimel

My father and I hardly spoke when he picked me up at the train station, nor during the long drive out to the farm through the snow-covered landscape. He'd recognized me instantly among the sea of young men who disembarked, waited patiently as I threaded my way to him through the crowd, pack slung over my shoulder. "Welcome home, son," he'd said, shaking my hand firmly, and I could tell by the tone of his voice and the force of his grip that he was real proud of me, and real glad to have me home alive once more. He didn't push at all, as we drove, no questions about what I would do now that the war was over, if I had ever killed a man, or how I felt to be home. All the questions I had been dreading during the long train ride from New York, when I wasn't thinking about her.

Staring at the bare trees that lined the road, I couldn't help worrying about her. Would everything be the same? So much might've happened: lightning, loggers, fire... I tried not to think about it, almost wished my father did ask me questions, anything to keep my mind from forming disaster scenarios.

But when we pulled up to the house, my worst fears were realized as I stared at the acres of barren furrows that stretched into land that, before I left, had been forest. I stepped out of the car, staring at all the missing trees. I was about to go racing off into the woods to make sure she was still there, make sure she was all right, when my mother saw me from the kitchen porch, came rushing out into the cold in just her house dress and apron to throw her arms about me. I kissed her, of course, took one last look at the forest over her shoulder as I hugged her tight, then dutifully followed her inside. But I couldn't help thinking about the forest the entire time, couldn't help worrying. I was quiet all through dinner, and even my sisters were subdued by my silence. Their quiet was noticeable since, in all the letters I'd gotten from home, Mother had written how they were at that age when then could talk a hole through a wall. I could feel my mother casting worried looks to my father. They thought it was the war, I knew, and were dying to ask me what was wrong. But they were afraid to. My mother wanted to take away my pain, make me the same happy boy I was before I left, and I loved her for it. But how could I tell them?

I wasn't thinking about the war at all. I was thinking about a tree and the woman who is its spirit: a woman whose eyes are filled with starlight; a woman whose hair is green in spring and summer, golden and red in fall; the woman who held my heart.

I kept my silence, letting them think it was the war that absorbed my thoughts, as I bided my time until I could rush out to the woods and see her.

* * *

As I ran along the familiar path after dinner, I couldn't help wondering if she had missed me as much as I had her, if she had missed me at all. I couldn't write her, as the other guys had done with their loves. She couldn't read, had never learned because she was so pained by the trees that were made into paper. And even if she could, I'd no way of getting a letter to her. Where was I to send it, 14th oak behind the McLeran's farm, General Delivery, Pine Plains, New York? I kept to myself and, when the other guys got letters from their loves, read them aloud to the rest of us, and showed off the locks of yellow, red, brown, or black; I thought of the four leaves I kept pressed between the pages of a book of poems by Wordsworth. I made whistles from the hats of her acorns, played slow and lonely songs on them in the evenings, as I thought of her.

Snow crunched under my feet as I ran beneath the bare, skeletal trees. Their long, moonlit shadows cut across my path like solid bars trying to prevent me from reaching her. I ran faster, desperate to see her again. I knew I couldn't really see her now, that she was dormant until Spring, but I needed to at least see her tree. I needed to see if she had left a sign of some sort, that she was still safe. That she still loved me.

My heart pounded with the exertion and anticipation as I ran along the last curve of the path before her tree. I cried out with relief when I saw that it was still whole and upright. I paused to catch my breath after my run and, standing in the snow as I stared at her tree, I felt warm with love. Her branches were covered with hundreds of yellow ribbons, fluttering like leaves in the moonlight.

The Seedling

John Higgins

(Session 2 – shift and shimmer)

Dr. Cummings looked up from her notepad and peered over the reading glasses straddling her nose. "Imagine a bridge, Steven. Right now, it's miles long. You will cross it and find understanding along the way; on the other side is peace."

Steven huddled in an overstuffed chair, legs pulled up to his chest. In another setting, he would have felt ridiculous—a thirty-four-year-old man curled in a chair like a child. But here, he was encouraged to remain comfortable and calm. Do what feels natural, she had said in the first session.

This was natural—clenched like a fist.

"OK."

"Are you still losing weight?"

"I'm not eating much, but I don't know if I can lose much more."

Dr. Cummings regarded him and made a note. *Emaciated, almost skeletal.*

Silence settled in the room like a cloud passing in front of the sun.

Steven let his gaze wander throughout the psychiatrist's office. It was only his second session, so there were many things to discover. Clocks were on every wall and others in varying size, digital and analog, crouched on tables and shelves. Knickknacks cluttered the room like forgotten dreams—sculptured characters and abstractions, buildings sealed in snow globes, various boats adorning a shelf all on their own—and, directly across from Steven, hanging behind Dr. Cummings' head was a three-foot-by-three-foot painting of a tree. It stood in a winterscape, surrounded by snowy hills and standing on a small island where an icy brook flowed on both sides, looping the trunk on both sides before joining into a singular stream on the other side.

In spite of the scene being winter, the tree was lush and green. Its leaves shaded with whites and silver to give the illusion of shivering in a frigid breeze.

"How have you been since our last session?" she asked quietly.

"OK, I guess."

"Have you reached any conclusions about what we talked about?"

"It feels like it was a dream."

"But if it had been a dream," she tapped her pen on her pad, "you wouldn't be here with me."

Steven grunted and pulled his legs closer to his chest. His denim jeans were rough and stiff against the inside of his forearms. The fabric was new, but he didn't remember having new jeans. In fact, he couldn't remember how he had gotten here. "Is *this* a dream?" He looked again at the trinkets and decorations that cluttered the office, neatly placed and varied, orderly but still felt chaotic, like a busy city street frozen in time.

"Why do you say that?" She peered over her reading glasses.

"This place is familiar, but alien... like in a dream. The things you have here—the statues, the painting, the pictures—I think I've seen them before."

"Well," she gestured toward the room with the pen. "Have a look around and find something that looks familiar."

Steven pursed his lips and let his gaze scan the room again. There was a doll in a glass case nestled in a corner that made him pause. The doll stood about a foot tall and had flowing brown hair, spilling from her scalp and settling on her shoulders like a cloak.

He unfurled himself from the chair and crossed the room. Figurines made from glass, metal, and wood lined the shelves in this part of the office, but only this porcelain doll resided in the protection of a glass case. The case was on a marble pedestal, about four feet high.

Steven touched the glass; it was so cold that he unconsciously flinched. There was no obvious way to open the case. "What's this one?"

"You tell me."

Dr. Cummings voice was oddly distant, but Steven didn't turn toward her. Instead, he leaned in close to the glass and peered into the doll's deep blue eyes, radiant against her alabaster skin.

"Rachel." He dropped his gaze to the floor. "She was the last one."

I walked to the head of the stairway. I was a young man—thirteen and nearly six feet tall. "He'll be a big 'un" Father usually said. "A big 'un, like his grandad. Tall and thin, a stalk with legs."

It was dark, here at the top of the stairs. The landing overlooked the living room below; the couch, chairs, and television were no more than smoky shadows in the feeble moonlight that seeped through the dirty windows.

I heard them walking, like they always did in the deep night. Father locked my bedroom door, but sometimes he would drink too much and forget. As the years progressed, he drank more often and would forget to lock my bedroom door more nights than not.

Many nights, I had seen them in the yard after they left the house. The hall window gave an excellent view of the yard, neatly mowed to the treeline. Mother's garden of herbs and flowers lined one side, meticulously tended in the summer, while the leaves of the nearby, dense copse of oaks shifted and shimmered in the humid breeze.

At night the flowers closed and bent their heads, as if in prayer... or perhaps to close their eyes to things that left the house and walked to the trees. I watched them walk side-by-side, their gait becoming more wobbly and forced, until they came within a few feet of the trees.

Then they dropped to all fours and scampered up into the trees and out of sight, embraced by the dark boughs.

Dr. Cummings tapped her pen against the pad and Steven found himself again in the chair, curled in on himself: legs gripped by his arms and fingers interlocked.

A thin smile creased her face.

(Session 7, boughs above and below)

My father knew I was watching them at night; I could tell by his silence at breakfast. Mother, too. There was tension on this day, the last day of my childhood. I had watched them for years, but today... today, I could feel the change in the air.

Mother slid the plate in front of me without a word. A single slab of meat lay there: bloody, barely warm.

"It's not cooked," I said.

"It's time you started eating like a big boy," Father said without lifting his eyes from his own bloody steak.

I looked at Mother, and her jaw clenched, causing the muscles to bulge in her cheeks. Her eyes narrowed as she shifted her gaze to her husband. "We need more," she said and sat at the table.

Father nodded and smiled. He popped a cut of raw, red meat into his mouth and looked me square in the eyes. "Time to go shopping." He still had that grin as he mashed the flesh with wet smacks of his teeth.

"How does this memory make you feel?" Dr. Cummings said.

Steven shook his head. "I don't know. I guess it felt good, like I was finally part of the family."

"What do you mean?"

"He never looked at me that way... like, *happy*. You know? There was a light in his eyes."

She scribbled something on the pad and tapped the pen twice. "What did he mean by 'shopping'?"

Steven flattened his lips into a tight seam. He looked up at the wall behind Dr. Cummings and studied the tree painting again. In the leaves, clinging to the branches, Steven could make out a Cheshire grin and dimly shining eyes that hung in the deep shadow like tarnished pennies.

Of course, it was there. Why hadn't he seen it before?

"My parents took in foster kids. Other times, Father would bring home whatever he could find."

"This is 'shopping'?" She jotted again and tilted her head. "What do you remember about it?"

"I usually didn't see them. I was locked in my room, most of the time. Sometimes, I would pass them on the way to the bathroom or maybe in the hall when I was headed down for dinner."

"And the other meals? Did you see them then?"

"We only ate dinner. That was the rule. 'Eating more often makes you fat and stupid,' Father would say." Steven pulled his legs close to his chest. "We were lean. He said that was how it had to be."

"When you said it was 'the last day of your childhood,' what did you mean?"

"That night, they let me walk with them. He let me *see*."

"Let you see what?"

Steven clucked his tongue once and shifted in his chair. His gaze cascaded away from the doctor and drifted to the knick-knacks. Painted figurines lined a shelf behind her desk, next to the painting of the tree. They were lined up like soldiers for review.

He slid from the chair and went to the shelf. Each figurine was childlike, cherubic: painted in bright colors, but with dour, even somber, expressions. Their clothes were earth tones, and ragged.

"Phillip," Steven pointed at one of the figures. "Ellie, Theresa, Conner, and..." he tapped on the last one, a boy in torn jeans and greasy sweatshirt. He was either yawning or screaming. "Marcus?" Steven tilted his head quizzically. "That doesn't sound right."

Dr. Cummings turned her head and tapped her pen twice on the notepad. "Matthew."

Steven nodded. "Of course. How could I forget?"

"Those were the other children in the house," she turned away and made a note.

He looked again at each figurine closely. "It breaks my heart every time I think about them," he whispered. "They trusted me. One by one, they trusted me. They thought I was one of them, a kid—yet another foster child."

"But you weren't," Dr. Cummings said and raised her eyes, looking only at the empty chair where Steven had been sitting.

Steven shook his head. "No. Each of them trusted me... until they were taken—and then, they knew who I really was. I saw it in their eyes."

Teeth, shark-like and sharp clamped down on Phillip, Ellie, Theresa, Conner, Matthew. Mouths came in, slavering, hungry, vicious. The creatures were black, wiry things with oily skin that refracted the meager moonlight. Their heads were broad and ovular with a row of yellow nodules that served as eyes; beneath the eyes was a broad, lipless grin of angular teeth.

Their six legs were spindly, needle-like, and ended in serrated pincers that gripped the limbs of the trees as they scampered down in a frenzy to feast on the sacrifice. The creatures ripped away small bits at a time, never killing quickly: savoring the delicate flesh. The victims writhed and shrieked through gagged mouths, flailing at the ones who devour.

"Suffering makes for sweet meat," Father said. "And fear is the gravy."

"And?" said Dr. Cummings with expectation. "Do you remember what happened next?"

Steven ground his teeth. "One of them tore open the body and crawled inside, greedily slurping at the innards until there was nothing but a shell of bones and skin. All the others were quiet and watched as the one who cleaned out the corpse folded itself into the cadaver, pulling the skin over it like a blanket." He sighed. "The others dug a hole and buried it, while it twitched inside the corpse."

She jotted in her notebook. "And your parents?"

"Mother was there... and Father. They were always there, standing behind me. I remember once, I turned toward him and he grinned at me. So much joy. The smile stretched across his face; it split his skin as the grin wrapped all the way back to his ears." Steven dropped his head. "Oh, Jesus. His teeth. I remember now. His teeth, jagged and yellow—like the others. And the oily, black face that ripped through that grin."

(Session 8, Trunk and roots)

Steven was crying, but no tears came. It was as if he had awoken from a nightmare of deep sadness while curled into the doctor's overstuffed chair. He looked up and saw Dr. Cummings waiting, gently tapping the back of her pen on the paper.

"Calm yourself, Steven," she said. "You're so close."

"How did I get here?" He straightened up and put his feet on the ground.

She smiled. "You never left. You never do."

"What do you mean?"

She set her notebook on a side-table and gestured behind Steven. "You're ready."

He stood and turned. Behind him was a wall of trees: dense, tall oaks crowded together and extending into darkness. Black, oily figures moved in the branches above, rustling leaves as they descended.

"Rachel," the doctor said from behind Steven. "You remember her. That's good."

Steven turned and Dr. Cummings was standing, bent forward, back hunched. Black claws erupted from the palm of each of her hands. A smile split across her face, tearing a gash in her cheeks, revealing a mouthful of pointed teeth pushing her human teeth aside.

"She's yours," the thing said as Dr. Cummings' face split and fell away. "Your first."

A scream slashed through the woods behind him.

He could smell her fear. Rachel's fear. The child screamed again and the creatures in the trees scampered down.

A tingle ran through Steven's body. She screamed again.

A grin stretched across his face.

Golden Oldies

Christine Collier

As usual Fred Brimmer listened to the golden oldies radio station as he and his son traveled to his daughter's house. He cranked the volume but still had a hard time hearing. He was too old to drive anymore or so *they* said. The *idiots,* as he called such people, took his license away when he turned ninety. Just because he wiped out their stupid mailbox a couple times. It was way too close to the driveway anyway and needed to be moved. How he missed his red truck.

Fred's daughter was having their last family picnic under the big oak tree by the creek in her yard. Family folklore shared that this oak tree had been planted the day Fred Brimmer was born. This was proven by a dated picture of Fred's father planting it. Another picture showed his mother and him with the caption, *Frederick and his mother, born at home, five hours old.* This picture had the same date as the tree planting. But now this stately oak had to come down as most of it was diseased and about to fall. For everyone's safety, professionals were hired, and it would be done that afternoon. They would say goodbye with one last picnic beneath its broad leaves. Fred often worried, when the young children were baiting their minnow traps in the creek, that a branch could fall on them.

He smiled when one of his favorite songs came on the radio. It told the story of a man getting out of prison after three years and he was coming home on a bus. He hoped to be reunited with the woman he loved but wasn't sure what she wanted. He wrote her a letter saying if she wanted him back to tie a yellow ribbon around the old oak tree in their neighborhood. He was afraid to even glance out the bus window and asked the driver to look for him. Fred chuckled, *what would have happened if there hadn't been a ribbon on that tree? The song said he would stay on the bus and put the blame on himself.* But luckily there were one hundred yellow ribbons around the old oak tree and the whole damn bus was cheering when they saw it was covered! He was coming home.

The next song on the radio was another one he loved about a man dreaming about the green, grass of home. Fred knew it was a tear jerker and too emotional for his son so he turned the volume down a bit. This song mentioned an old oak tree too and that this man used to play on it as a child near his house with the cracked and dried paint. As an adult, it tells how he is surrounded by four gray walls on death row, with a guard and an old padre at his side. Sadness enters this ballad when it mentions his mama and papa and his sweet Mary, with hair of gold and lips like cherries, coming to say goodbye to him in his dream. For he knew that he would soon be buried beneath the green, green grass of home. *Funny, how often old oak trees play a part in songs and stories of life. Now, today, it even will for me.* Fred felt a tear trickle from the corner of his eye, and he quickly brushed it aside.

The dogs burst into loud barking and insanity as they drove into the driveway. The outdoor farm table under the oak tree was already set with a tablecloth and bowls of covered food. It looked like planks from the tree service were piled on the side of the driveway. Fred had a hard time getting out of the car. He felt very lame and almost tripped when he took a step. His daughter rushed to hug him and kiss his cheek.

"Dad, the tree cutters are coming at three so we will start eating right away."

"Sounds good to me. That tree is huge. I want to see it come down as I don't want it to harm anyone."

"We will watch from the front porch with a glass of fresh lemonade and strawberry shortcake."

"I was inside this house ninety-two years ago as a new baby, and now as an old man I'll be on the front porch." They all settled in at the table under the tree.

"That's right Dad. So many years have gone by. Would you like fried chicken, potato salad and some corn on the cob?"

"Sounds good honey, but a small piece of chicken and just a dab of salad. Feeling tired today plus I'll need room for the strawberry shortcake."

Fred sat at the table and stared at the old tree and was amazed to see a ribbon tied around it. "Why is that yellow ribbon around that tree?" He questioned his daughter and seemed worried and afraid.

"The tree cutters did it when they dropped off the scaffolding and chains, but I'm not sure why, It's the only tree coming down and they've checked it out several times. It's not like our tree needs to be singled out from a large group."

After dinner they all went on the porch to get out of the sun. The tree service people came and moved everything and told them to stay far away. Fred's daughter asked the foreman why he had placed a yellow ribbon around the tree.

"It has many meanings to different people, but our company uses a yellow ribbon all the time because one meaning is that a loved one is returning home."

"I love that meaning. Hope the job goes smoothly."

Fred watched every minute of the tree removal. The earth shuddered when the biggest part of the trunk slammed to the ground. The yellow ribbon broke in two as it hit, and at that very moment Fred quietly slumped over in his chair. His plate fell to the ground. He had returned home for good.

Black-eyed Susan

Delfina Hex

There is this one special tree in our woods, well really it is two trees growing so close that their roots and branches have merged in places. Anyway, the resulting formation looks like a window. And I swear, once I saw a butterfly go in one side and NOT out the other. It just disappeared in the opening. Nobody believes me, but I know what I saw.

I like to pretend the window is a gate to another world, one kinder than the one I live in. The boys always laugh and say another world would just as likely be worse. They say only babies believe in fairy tales and magic gateways. Today they emphasized their point by throwing rocks through the opening before they ran off.

I am the only one to notice that the last rock didn't land. I don't want the other side to think our world holds only rocks and rock throwers, so I pick a bouquet of wildflowers and carefully toss it through the opening. It just spills across the ground beyond—how many rocks had the boys tossed before the one that didn't land? I don't know, but I'm not about to give up.

I take apart the bouquet and began to toss through one flower at a time. I have to stop when it gets too dark to see. Walking home, I wonder if the gate is closed forever—because of the rocks—and I cry. I should have known better. At home, they give me something to cry about. But I don't care.

The next chance I get, I rob the neighbor's garden of blossoms—brighter, prettier than the glorified weeds I had tossed through before. Maybe my flowers hadn't been pretty enough or special enough. I pay dearly for those stolen blooms, and they don't even work.

Now that I can walk again, I'm starting over with what wildflowers I can find: Goldenrod, Queen Anne's Lace, and other, daisy-like plants—proud names for humble blooms. I'm tossing flowers so fast I almost miss seeing one disappear. It's the Black-eyed Susan—funny, that is what the boys call me. Surely that is a good sign.

The boys must have told the folks about my tree. I can hear angry voices calling my name and people crashing through the brush. There's not much time. I back up to get a running start. The portal isn't all that big, so I'll have to dive through headfirst.

I hope it works.

The Secrets Trees Keep

Matt McGee

"Did I ever tell you about the super-ball I lost as a kid?"

Evan rolled his eyes.

His dad wasn't going to tell a story again, was he?

But then something clicked. Call it maturity, even though Evan was only 14. All of a sudden, he realized his dad wasn't going to be around forever. There would come a day, probably a long, long time from now, when his dad wouldn't be able to regale him with a seemingly endless, pointless story.

Yet here came another one.

And they always seemed to point Evan in a direction he needed to go.

Evan put his elbow on the arm of the couch and set his cheek against his fist. "No. I don't think I know the super-ball story."

"Well as you know, I grew up in a nice little house in Upstate New York. It was awesome. You haven't lived until you've slept in a top bunk bed, right up next to the ceiling during a thunderstorm. Whoa!

It's like everyone in heaven is up there bowling in an alley right over your head."

"Cool. So... what's this got to do with losing a super-ball?"

Evan's dad was getting up there in age. Almost forty. Evan had to keep him on track.

"I'm getting to that, smart guy. So your grandfather and grandmother, they bought this house and it had this great, big maple tree out front. Shed its leaves every year, like a carpet of gold and red and yellows. Then my dad, your grandfather..."

Evan sighed. "Why do you always do that?"

His dad seemed surprised at the interruption. It derailed his train of thought.

"What? Do what?"

"You always say, '*My father, your grandfather,*' like I can't make the connection. Just say, '*My dad* or *your grandfather*.' Either way, I totally get who you mean."

"Sheesh. Okay." Evan's dad thought a moment. "Where was I?"

"Maple tree."

"Right! Carpet of red and yellow and greens, like a traffic light had shot out a million little leaves in its own colors."

"Wow. That's descriptive. Okay, so. Super-ball."

"We didn't have a lot of money. Not like now, your mom being a doctor and all. She brings home the bacon, boy..."

"Super-ball," Evan reminded.

"Right. We didn't have a lot of dough. But occasionally, if I looked around and kept my eyes peeled—you know, looked under soda machines and stuff—I might occasionally find a stray coin someone had dropped and given up on. And this one day I found a quarter. And what did I do with it?"

"Bought a super-ball," Evan guessed.

"Bought a super-ball. Absolutely. The grocery store at the bottom of our hill had a gumball machine full of them. And for a quarter I scored one. It wasn't exactly orange or yellow, but more of a tangerine color."

"That's great." Evan opened the guide on the TV. *American Pickers* was coming on.

Evan wanted to watch it. But with his dad nearby, it was a dangerous move. More than once, Evan had been watching the show and one of the guys would find something old in a storage locker somewhere. They'd declare it was worth a jillion dollars and his dad would shout, "Oh my God, I used to have one of those! I should've kept it!"

Old people were annoying like that.

"Anyway," his dad got back on track, "the best part of this super-ball? It smelled great. Like some kind of chemical factory had made it."

"They probably did."

"Also, I'd bought it with my own money..."

"Money you found."

"Which I found on my own. And most of all, this thing bounced like no other super-ball I'd ever seen."

"Maybe you just thought it was better because it was yours," Evan played along.

"No, no. Those other super-balls were like... you know those balls that come on the end of the paddle and you bang it back and forth? It's attached with a string?"

Evan remembered seeing something like that at a toy store when he was a kid. "Yeah."

"Most super-balls were like that. The worst. I mean, all full of air bubbles, just the worst."

The commercials were ending. The show would be on in a moment.

"OK," Evan nudged his dad along, "what's this got to do with the maple tree?"

"I'm out bouncing this ball one day. In the street. It's getting dark. Suddenly the thing takes an odd bounce, and I couldn't be sure because it was getting dark, but it seemed to have bounced into the maple tree. I waited 'til the next day and climbed the tree."

"Grandpa let you do that?"

"He encouraged it. And I was a champ. Any time you wanna climb a tree, let me know," his dad said proudly. "Anyway, climbed the tree.

No ball. Didn't see it on the ground anywhere. Maybe it was higher up? I don't know. I finally gave up."

"Aww."

"Story isn't over."

The previews for the show were coming on. "Of course it isn't."

"What?"

"What," Evan answered. "Dad," he gestured at the TV.

"Got it. Anyway, here's the gist of the whole thing, Okay? Years later, just before you were born, I revisited the house. Part of the tree had fallen the night before. Guys with chainsaws were there. As I watched them cut up the limbs to haul away, I look..."

"And there's your ball," Evan guessed.

"Yeah! The tree? It had grown around it!"

Evan muted the show. It was a repeat anyway.

"OK, wait. You're saying your ball bounced up into the tree and the tree grew around it?"

"Yeah!"

"Like swallowed it up?"

"Kinda. It had sorta lodged in a Y-shape branch, and that branch became a whole limb. The bark sorta surrounded it over the years. Like the tree was holding the ball for me all that time."

"So'd you get it back?"

"Heck yeah! One of the guys went to his work truck and came back with a screwdriver. We pried that sucker outta there. Didn't bounce real good but hey, whadda ya want after all those years stuck in a maple tree?"

Evan nodded.

"That's a great story, Dad." But really, Evan was thinking: *This is a metaphor for old people. They might look like every other tree around, but who knows what secrets they hold under their bark?*

His dad nodded triumphantly. "Hey, who knows. Maybe someday you'll lose something in a tree too, and you can tell your kids about it."

* * *

But in fact, Evan had lost something in a tree.

And not too long ago.

Evan lay awake that night, thinking over the possibilities. *Could it still be up there? What if someone else found it before he could climb the tree and look for the evidence?* He tried not to think about it.

But it kept him awake. He replayed the events of that evening over and over again in his head.

He and Chrissy had grown up together. She'd lived in a two-story house halfway down the block, while Evan and his family lived in the cul-de-sac. He and Chrissy had played together, learned to ride bikes together, taken swimming lessons, and played soccer together. If Evan wasn't at her house after school, she was at his. They knew other kids in the neighborhood of course, but mostly they just hung out with each other.

When they went off to spend the day at the lake, Chrissy was invited. "Tell your little friend to come along!" his mother would cheer.

His *little friend*? What did that even mean?

They were eleven when Chrissy came to his house one evening after dinner. His dad had answered the door.

"Chrissy! What are you doing out after dark?"

Chrissy had looked over her shoulder. "It just got dark. Supper's not ready yet. Is Evan here?"

Evan's dad looked over his own shoulder. "Yeah, he's here. Evan! After you two talk, go on right home, okay? I don't want your parents worried."

"Oh, they know I'm here."

"Okay, I..."

Evan dashed up to the door. "Hey Chrissy. 'Sup?"

His dad slid away. "I'll leave you two to talk."

She and Evan watched him go into the den. It was only ten feet away.

"Can you talk a sec?"

"Yeah." Evan stepped out, taking the doorknob in hand. "Dad, we're gonna be out front!"

"Don't go far."

Evan had rolled his eyes. "Sheesh. Like I'm going to get lost going out to the driveway."

"My mom's the same way," Chrissy said as they walked down the driveway. Streetlights had popped on. Their orange bulbs gave Chrissy a sort of glow. With the branches of the small tree beside the driveway throwing shadows across her face, Chrissy looked like a girl in a movie. She looked down. Her tone shifted serious.

"Um. Look. My dad is out of town, but he just called during dinner. He got a new job in Minnesota."

"Bummer. Where is that?"

"Almost in Canada. It's supposed to be really green. Lots of lakes and snow and fresh air. Dad says we'll love it. Anyway, his company offered him a bunch of money and, well, whatever. So, we're moving."

"That sucks. When?"

"End of the week."

"*What*?"

"Yeah. Mom already put our house on the market. She says it's a really good time to sell, we're gonna make a bunch of money, blah blah blah. She's all on board about this."

"What's your dad think?"

"He's already there. Staying in some big hotel. We're gonna join him at the end of the week."

"Sheesh."

"Yeah."

"So."

"So yeah," she said. "He sent us this FedEx package? You know, with all these little tchotckes in it."

"Little what?" Evan looked confused.

"Tchotckes. You never heard that?"

"No."

"Like little trinkets. And toys. Little... jewelry and stuff."

"Okay."

"You know how like if you go to your grandma's house and she's got like a million little figurines?"

"Yeah," Evan admitted.

"Tchotckes," Chrissy said.

"Got it."

She was stalling. "So. He sent me this. I wanted you to have it."

She handed him a little gold necklace. "The pendant," she pointed, "it's shaped like Minnesota. He thought I'd like it. But . . ."

Evan looked at the little charm. If he turned it sideways, he thought it looked like a bowtie.

"I thought I'd give it to you," Chrissy said. "You know. As a reminder."

"Of what?"

Chrissy acted like she wanted to say something else. "That if you ever get bored, or lonely, or need a friend? Come to Minnesota."

They talked a while longer. Neither one wanted to go back inside. He felt like he was never going to see her again. Of course they can call and text, she'd said. But he knew better. He watched as she walked back to her house.

It wasn't going to be the same.

Evan had stood there in place a while longer. How could her dad do this? How could everyone just go along with it? Weren't friends supposed to be forever? He looked at the little gold necklace. Somehow it reminded him of everything he didn't want to think about. Specifically, change.

He'd always hated change. The end of every school year meant he'd have to get used to a whole new classroom, sometimes a new school, or a whole new set of friends.

Friends. They were supposed to be forever.

Suddenly he was tense with anger. Evan had turned and swung his arm back. He threw the necklace as hard and as far as he could in the opposite direction. He stormed back into the house.

He slammed the door.

His dad looked up from the TV.

"Hey, you'll knock the house down for crying out loud!"

His dad was always coming up with little sayings like that. *For crying out loud.* Or *don't buy a pig in a poke!* What in the world did that even mean? Or his all-time favorite: *wherever you go, there you are!* Evan still hadn't figured that one out. Of course he was wherever he went. Where else would he be?

Evan stormed up to his room that night and plopped backward onto his bed. He let out a big sigh. He laid in place until long after dark. He got up only once, to look in the direction of where Chrissy' house was—for the moment anyway.

He looked at the streetlight, how it cast its orange glow on the neighborhood. The one at the curb out front of his house lit up the tree beside the driveway with a welcoming, almost buddy-like kind of glow—as if it were sympathetic to Evan losing his friend. And hey, if he wanted to rest a while, relax, come hang out here. Lean against me. Meanwhile, I've got things handled down here. For a moment the light seemed to be like a new best friend.

And just as he was about to turn away from the window, Evan glanced at the tree beside the driveway. He wasn't sure, but he thought he saw the faintest glint of light off something in the tree. It was probably just a wet leaf, but whatever it was shone like gold.

* * *

Evan walked out the door, down the driveway to the sidewalk. He looked both ways. He hadn't gone very far. But *wherever you go, there you are.*

Well, here he was.

And somehow, at the moment, he thought about his dad's superball.

He turned and took a couple steps up the driveway. The tree there had grown a little in the two years since Chrissy had left.

He looked up into its branches. And he thought of the little glimmer he'd seen that night, the tiny gold flash. A signal maybe, telling him that somewhere out there, he still had a friend.

Evan looked over each shoulder. He looked up and down the street. He walked over and grabbed the biggest branch in reach that the tree had to offer.

He started to climb.

Balming the Thorn

Vonnie Winslow Crist

Strange moon, thought Kylie as she wheeled Nana around the hawthorn tree rooted in the corner of the backyard. Luckily her grandmother weighed less than a hundred pounds, otherwise Kylie wasn't certain she could have managed to quickly circle the tree nine times on a muggy July evening. But Nana insisted that three times three was the magic number when participating in ancient ceremonies.

As Kylie leaned on the wheelchair handles and caught her breath, her grandmother gazed lovingly at the hawthorn. Nana was clothed in the same ivory gown with hawthorn leaves embroidered around its neckline and the edges of its sleeves which she'd worn to balm the thorn since her teens. The sturdy shoes and support hose visible below the gown's hem were the only change in her attire from those bygone days.

She studied her grandmother. The moonlight silvered Nana's hair, which was pulled back in a bun. It also caught in her eyes, giving them a youthful sparkle.

"It's beautiful," whispered Nana. She tilted her head back to admire the flowery garlands, ropes of leaves, and bright ribbons they'd hung on the tree's lower branches. "Your great-great grandmother balmed the thorn in England with her grandmother when she was a child."

"So you've said." Kylie patted her head. To please her grandmother, she'd braided her hair and slipped a sprig of rosemary behind her right ear, but her unruly curls were sure to break free.

"In those days, every town had a Guardian Tree. Oak, thorn, holly, birch, willow—it didn't matter, just that the tree was ancient and imbued with old magic."

"That was a long time ago, Nana."

Kylie sighed. She had lived with Nana since she'd graduated from high school and had assisted her in balming the thorn for three Julys now. For three summers, she had helped gather the greenery and blooms from the garden to weave into long strands for draping on the hawthorn. Each time, she'd cut silky ribbons into six-foot lengths to tie on the boughs. Then, she'd listened year after year to the same stories about how her ancestors had balmed the tree in Appleton Thorn.

"Guardian Trees are special," said Nana. "Their roots reach deep and out to the young trees around them. Guardians share nutrients and knowledge through the tiniest of their rootlets. When it is time for them to die, they give away all their life essence to the surrounding trees."

"Very generous." She glanced at her watch. A few more minutes of tree talk, and she would push her grandmother and her wheelchair inside.

"But they don't just protect their fellow trees."

Here comes the weird part, thought Kylie. As a Science-Education student, she believed in the inter-connectivity of many species in the forest. She also knew the planet needed trees to keep the air clean, assist in preventing erosion, and help with the climatic greenhouse effect. That said, she didn't for an instant buy into her grandmother's folklore. And she certainly wouldn't be sharing any of Nana's foolishness with her students when she began teaching in the autumn.

"Those who honor the Guardians will be remembered by the trees." Her grandmother sighed. "I wish I could spend the night in the garden, leaning against the hawthorn—my head resting on her trunk. Oh, what wonderful dreams I would have."

"I don't think that's a good idea in this neighborhood anymore. There's more crime than when you first moved here," Kylie replied, and swatted at an insect helping itself to a meal at her expense. She would have an itchy welt on her forearm by morning. The bigger worry was, who else was out after dark? "The mosquitoes are out. We need to head in."

No sooner had Kylie spoken when she heard a rustling in the shrubs.

"Where are you going, ladies?" asked a man as he stepped from behind the butterfly bush near the back door of the house.

Kylie turned her grandmother's wheelchair so they squarely faced the speaker.

"You are trespassing," Nana jabbed the air with a forefinger. "Leave my garden."

"Don't think so," replied the man as he stepped closer, blocking their way not only to the safety of the house, but to the cell phone Kylie had carelessly left on the porch.

Kylie tilted her head. There was something off about the man's appearance.

"Goblin," hissed her grandmother. "I've seen your kind creeping out from the culvert across the street."

"Nana, not now." The last thing Kylie needed to deal with was her grandmother's fixation on goblins sneaking into the city set on robbing and harassing the *regular people*. She studied the face of the person smirking at her. He looked like a man—a man with slightly irregular features, but a man nonetheless. Still, something subconsciously was telling Kylie that this man was *wrong* somehow. Maybe it was that his arms were too long, his hands too large, or that his lips were curled in a snarl. Maybe it was his mismatched, pointed ears.

"You shoulda minded your own business," warned the man. He cracked his knuckles for emphasis. "We can't have you spreading no tales. Somebody might take you seriously. That wouldn't do. It'd make it harder on us."

Us? Kylie's heart raced. Her skin goose-fleshed. *Did he just admit he was a goblin?* Kylie shook her head, trying to process what had been said. As the goblin-man took another step forward, she decided it didn't matter if he was a goblin or some other magical creature, he shouldn't be in Nana's yard.

Even if anyone nearby had their air conditioning off and windows open, she knew they would probably ignore any screams, assuming they came from some kids playing in the alley. *I can't call for help,* thought Kylie as she glanced at her phone on the porch behind the goblin. She shifted her grip on the wheelchair handles. *Nana isn't mobile enough to make a run for it. Which leaves me with a basic knowledge of karate and...* Kylie smiled before finishing her thought. *And a pair of small garden shears in my pocket.*

Despite two years of classes, Kylie wasn't a master of karate or of any other martial art. But desperate situations called for desperate measures. Glad she'd stayed attired in her tank top and loose-fitting pants rather than changing into a dress, Kylie pressed her lips together and moved from behind Nana.

"Don't, Kylie!" her grandmother cried as Kylie quickly stepped forward.

Ignoring her grandmother, she brought her left leg up as if preparing to snap it out in a kick. Next, quick as a snake-strike, she withdrew the garden shears from her pocket and lunged forward. With a loud, exhaled "Ha!" she shoved the steel blades between the ribs of the goblin.

The goblin gazed down at Kylie, a startled look on his dim-witted face.

For a split-second, the creature's flesh resisted the blades' thrust. With a final surge of strength she pushed once more and felt the blades sink in.

A blood-curdling wail came from the goblin. Whether from surprise or fear, Kylie stumbled back.

The goblin grunted, lowered his eyelids half-way down, and grinned. "It ain't so easy as that."

The mannish creature continued to grin as he pulled the offending shears from his chest. He tossed them over the wall that surrounded Nana's yard. The garden tool clattered as it struck the sidewalk, then bounced onto the cement surface of the alleyway.

With garden shears gone, it looked like her miserable karate skills would have to do. She focused on keeping her center of gravity low, her arms raised before her, and her fingers extended and pressed together.

My empty hands are weapons, she thought. *Weapons for defense. Weapons to protect Nana and me.* She knew that even if they somehow managed to get safely inside, their safety would be temporary.

As three more goblins slunk from around the corner of Nana's house and joined their wounded comrade, Kylie backed up until she was beside her grandmother. If this was the end for her, she wanted to be close to the most important person in her life. That's when she noticed the chanting.

Soft as a breeze rustling leaves, Nana was calling to her Guardian Tree for aid.

"Ain't going to help, old woman," jeered one of the new goblins. "Trees is deaf. Don't care no more about womenfolk."

A fifth goblin climbed over Nana's stone fence and into the backyard. He was bigger than the first four. Worse, he had a machete gripped tightly in his hand. "Let's get it over with," he snarled. "There's more than these two that needs killing tonight."

Terrified, Kylie knelt down beside her grandmother, clasped Nana's frail hands, and joined her in beseeching the hawthorn for assistance.

The goblins laughed and surged forward. Then they stopped, a look of horror frozen on their almost-human faces.

From behind and above Kylie and her grandmother, creaks and groans emanated from the hawthorn. The Guardian Tree leaned forward and grabbed the five goblins with branchy fingers. As Kylie watched, it wrapped its wooden appendages tightly around the squirming faeries. Then, the Guardian Tree's branches, down to the tiniest twig, constricted like snakes coiled around rats. As the branches continued to squeeze, the goblins opened their mouths to scream. But only gasping and gurgling noises came from the malformed creatures as they were crushed by the hawthorn. Kylie felt queasy when the crunches of breaking bones filled the air.

Too surprised to move or speak, all Kylie could do was hold onto Nana with her mouth open and eyes wide. A few seconds later, the goblins' limp bodies dangled above them.

Nana pulled her hands away from Kylie's and pressed them together as if in prayer. Her dark eyes sparkled as she whispered, "They are coming."

"Who?" Kylie couldn't imagine what was making the approaching drag-thump sounds.

"The Guardian Tree's charges," her grandmother replied as if it was the most obvious thing in the world. "The nearby younger trees are cared for by the Guardian Tree. Now, in the Guardian's time of need, the younger trees will come." Nana had barely gotten the word *charges* out when fifteen or sixteen pear trees marched up to the stone wall surrounding Nana's yard. Their awkward gait caused Kylie to look down. The trunks of the pear trees merged into a creeping mass of roots. The throng of younger trees stopped, then turned toward the hawthorn.

Kylie recognized the Bradford pear trees. They lined the sidewalk on this side of Monument Street, and offered shade to pedestrians as they went about their days. Pedestrians who chatted or texted on their phones as they hustled down Monument rarely, if ever, glanced at the Bradford pears. Without a word, the ancient hawthorn deposited the goblins into the outstretched limbs of the pear trees, and gestured toward the culvert located on the vacant lot across the road.

Kylie stood up, still dumbstruck, and watched as the Bradford pears' trunks bent slightly and the topmost branches lowered in a leafy bow. Next, the pear trees lumbered over to the lot. They tossed the broken goblins on the ground. Using their roots, the young trees tore the bodies apart until the deadly faeries were nothing but bloody pieces littering the dirt.

Even from across the street, Kylie not only saw the sheen of blood, but smelled the scent of it. Her stomach lurched as, using their roots like straws, the pear trees sucked the liquid from the fleshy bits. Thus, making certain they'd squelched tonight's goblin threat.

Still in a daze, but drawn to the carnage like a rubbernecker at an automobile accident, Kylie stumbled between the lavender bushes to the stonewall to get a better view of what would happen next.

After a nod in the direction of the Guardian hawthorn, most of the younger trees shuffled back to their square of earth and re-embedded their roots in the soil. The only evidence of their adventure was that the edges of nearby sidewalks were slightly raised and clumps of dirt were scattered on the walkway.

The remaining pear trees swept the dried goblin flesh, bones, and teeth into the culvert, then pushed several large rocks across the entrance. After bowing slightly to Nana's hawthorn, they, too, shuffled to their square of dirt and resumed their normal places in the landscape of the city.

That's when she tore her eyes away from the Bradford pear trees and noticed her grandmother. Nana was on her feet, holding onto one of the Guardian Tree's branches—dancing. The wheelchair was on its side. Nearby, lay Nana's orthopedic shoes.

As Kylie watched, her grandmother's support stockings slithered off and dropped to the ground. Her grandmother's bun had come undone allowing her hair to float around her face like a halo as she twirled to a tune Kylie couldn't hear. There were fireflies pulsing an eerie green light-show around Nana, and every plant in the yard had turned its blooms to face them.

Unwilling to break the spell that enchanted the backyard, Kylie stood still as the angel statue in Nana's garden and watched a miracle. This moment seemed the stuff of fairy tales, the heart of all the stories told to her by her grandmother. After a few minutes, Nana looked at her, smiled, let go of the hawthorn branch, and drifted to the ground like dandelion fluff.

Kylie rushed forward, knelt, and lifted her grandmother's head into her lap.

"I'm leaving," whispered Nana.

Kylie brushed wild strands of white hair back from Nana's face, then took her frail hand. "Don't be silly. We'll get you back into your chair and inside."

"Not this time," Nana sighed. She squeezed Kylie's hand. "Now, it will be up to you to watch for goblins and balm the thorn."

"Anything you say," she promised as she tried to help her grandmother sit up. "Come on, there's a cup of tea with your name on it waiting..."

"No, dearest," said Nana. She reached out and touched Kylie's cheek. "They have come for me. You must let me go."

Before Kylie could protest, hundreds of twinkling fireflies landed on her grandmother, then lifted up in unison, and flew through the hawthorn's limbs. And for a moment, amid the flowery garlands, ropes of leaves, and bright ribbons they'd hung earlier on the hawthorn's lower branches, Kylie saw Nana laughing.

As she watched, her mother's mother grew thin as mist and sailed skyward with the fireflies. She glanced down at the tired body she cradled, and knew without checking for a heartbeat or exhaled breath that Nana was gone.

"You are not alone," the hawthorn seemed to whisper. "I am here."

Before she went inside to deal with Nana's passing and begin the grieving process, Kylie rested her head against the Guardian's trunk. She breathed deeply the magical scents of the flowers, closed her eyes, and dreamed the most wonderful dreams.

The Loneliest Tears

Michael H. Hanson

The forest was born from the acorns of the first tree whose roots grew deep through boulders of antiquity.

It spread across the base of the father of mountains cutting wound-like furrows with the winds and the rains and birthing the mother of all of Earth's valleys.

Burrowing through the soil is the very first song and the words of the song gave voice to mankind's fiery dawn.

Near the end of time all of the trees will reach each other and branch will embrace branch in one grand vale.

The wind and the forest will wed beneath a red sun and all of life's whispers will combine into one mighty shout.

All of the forest's incandescent leaves will be shed and fall like the universe's loneliest tears.

Authors Biographical Information

Dawn Vogel's academic background is in history, so it's not surprising much of her fiction is set in earlier times. Her steampunk series, *Brass and Glass*, is available from DefCon One Publishing. She lives in Seattle with her husband, author Jeremy Zimmerman, and their herd of cats. Visit her: http://historythatneverwas.com.

Adam Meyer is a Shamus award nominee whose short fiction has appeared in *Malice Domestic: Murder Most Theatrical, Crime Travel, The Beat of Black Wings* and other anthologies. He has upcoming stories in *Mickey Finn 3, Groovy Gumshoes* and more. His TV credits include several Lifetime movies and true-crime series for Investigation Discovery and A&E. He recently wrote his first thriller, *Missing Rachel*, and is the author of the YA novel *The Last Domino*.

Sarah M. Lewis now writes under the name **Leonora Lewis**. She figures the name her Grandma Lewis hated has to be good for something. Her poetry took 1st and 3rd place in the August 2011 Writers' Journal Poetry Contest. Her fiction has appeared in Thuggish Itch: Birds Have Teeth, Wyldblood, and COLP: Feet. She lives in southeast Texas and is an active member of the Woodlands Writing Guild.

Lawrence Schimel (New York, 1971) writes in both Spanish and English and has published over one hundred twenty books as author or anthologist, in a wide range of genres, including fiction, poetry, graphic novels & children's literature. Some of his children's books have been translated into English, including *Let's Go See Papá*!, illustrated by Alba Rivera Marina (Groundwood) and the board books *Early One Morning and Bedtime,* Not *Playtime*, both illustrated by Elina Braslina (Orca). He is also the editor or co-editor of anthologies L*ike Streets* *of Blood: Vampire Stories from New York City* (Cumberland House), *Things Invisible to See* (Circlet), or *Tarot Fantastic* (DAW). He is also a prolific literary translator. His translations into Spanish include the graphic novel *They Called us Enemy* by George Takei (Top Shelf) and picture book *Millions of Cats* by Wanda Gàg (Libros del Zorro Rojo); his translations into English include the middle grade novels *The Wild Book* by Juan Villoro (Restless Books) and *The Treasure of Barracuda* by Llanos Campos (Sourcebooks). He lives in Madrid, Spain, where he founded the Spanish chapter of the Society of Children's Book Writers & Illustrators and served as Regional Advisor for 5 years.

Daniel Klim is a 21-year-old writer from Illinois. His favorite writers include Gillian Flynn, Nas, and Paul Thomas Anderson. He is always open to book recommendations from fellow readers.

Eric Fritz is a speculative fiction writer, web developer, and amateur bartender with work previously appearing in *Every Day Fiction* and *Martian*. He is ambivalent towards our new robot overlords. You can find him digitally at @CommonHeresy on Twitter and physically in Cambridge, where he lives with a plush cat named Will.

Vonnie Winslow Crist, SFWA, HWA, is author of Beneath Raven's Wing, The Enchanted Dagger, Owl Light, The Greener Forest, and other books. Her writing has been published in *Amazing Stories, Cast of Wonders, Faerie Magazine, Mythica, Weird Sisters, Merrow, Fae Wings and Hidden Things, Insignia 2020: Best Asian Speculative Fiction, Best Indie Speculative Fiction: 2018*, and elsewhere. Believing the world is still filled with mystery, magic, and miracles, Vonnie strives to celebrate the power of myth in her writing. For more information: http://www.vonniewinslowcrist.com

Kevin Hopson has dabbled in many genres over the years, but crime fiction and fantasy are his true loves. His novelette, *Pursuing the Dead*, was a 2019 Author Shout Reader Ready Awards winner. And if you're a fan of light fantasy, check out *The Emperor's Guar*d series. You can learn more about Kevin by visiting his website athttp://www.kmhopson.com.

Ray Daley was born in Coventry & still lives there. He served six years in the RAF as a clerk & spent most of his time in a Hobbit hole in High Wycombe. He is a published poet & has been writing stories since he was ten. His current dream is to eventually finish the *Hitch Hikers* fanfic novel he's been writing since 1986. Tweet him @RayDaleyWriter

Victory Witherkeigh is a female Filipino/PI author originally from Los Angeles, CA, currently living in the Las Vegas area. She has print publications in the horror anthologies Supernatural Drabbles of Dread through Macabre Ladies Publishing, Bodies Full of Burning through Sliced Up Press, and In Filth It Shall Be Found through OutCast Press. Her first novel, set to debut in December 2022 with Cinnabar Moth Publishing, has been a finalist for Killer Nashville's 2020 Claymore Award, a 2020 Cinnamon Press Literature Award Honoree, and long-listed in the 2021 Voyage YA Book Pitch Contest.

John Higgins has a degree in English, lives with his wife and twin daughters in the Poconos. He's written a novel, *Soulscape* and has had a few short stories published in collections, including "*Crypt Gnat*s," and "*WhoDunI*t." He took a ten-year break from fiction writing because it crushed his soul, but got better.

Kevin Brown has had Fiction, Non-fiction and Poetry published in over 100 Literary Journals, Magazines and Anthologies. Brown has won numerous writing competitions and fellowships and was nominated for multiple prizes and awards, including three Pushcart Prizes.

Christine Collier is the author of many books including a four book cozy mystery series. Excerpts from her children's chapter books are used for school testing and assessment by Measured Progress. Her writing is included in many themed, fiction, and nonfiction anthology books. She's been published in various magazines and a regular contributor to a family newspaper magazine.

Gargi Mehra works as a Project Manager in the IT arm of an international bank. Her work has appeared in numerous literary magazines online and in print, including *The Forge Literary Magazine*, *The Temz Review*, *The Writer*, among others. She lives in Pune, India with her husband and two children. She blogs at www.gargimehra.com.

Delfina Hex is a pen name used by Betsy A. Riley. She is a multi-genre author, artist, and poet who uses several pen names. She grew up in Murray Kentucky, then worked more than three decades at Oak Ridge National Laboratory in Tennessee before moving to Maryland to take a job with the Federal government. She began marketing her creative writing in 2011 and since has published poems, short stories, and artwork in periodicals and anthologies. Betsy was the Presidential Scholar from Kentucky in 1970 and has a bronze medal from President Richard M. Nixon.

Matt McGee writes short fiction in the Los Angeles area. In 2020 his stories appeared in *Barrelhouse, Sage* and *Gnashing Teeth.* When not typing he drives around in rented cars and plays goalie in local hockey leagues.

Mark Towse is an Englishman living in Australia. He would sell his soul to the devil or anyone buying if it meant he could write full-time. Alas, he left it very late to begin this journey, penning his first story since primary school at the ripe old age of 45. Since then, he's been published in the likes of Flash Fiction Magazine, T*he Dread Machine, Cosmic Horror, Suspense Magazine, ParABnormal, Raconteur*, and his work has also appeared on many exceptional podcasts such as *The Grey Rooms, No Sleep, Creepy, Tales to Terrify*, etc. His first collection, *'Face the Music*,' was released by *All Things That Matter* Press His debut novella, '*Nana*,' was published by D&T Publishing in March, also available via the usual outlets.

James Blakey's fiction has appeared in *Mystery Weekly*, *Crimson Streets,* and O*ver My Dead Body*. His story '*The Bicycle Thief*' won a 2019 Derringer Award. He lives in the Shenandoah Valley where he writes full-time. When James isn't writing, he can be found on the hiking trail—he's climbed forty of the fifty US state high points—or bike-camping his way up and down the East Coast. Find him at www.JamesBlakeyWrites.com.

Matthew (Matt) Hughes writes fantasy, space opera, and crime fiction. He has sold 24 novels to publishers large and small in the UK, US, and Canada, and more than 90 works of short fiction to professional markets.

Shari Held is an Indianapolis-based fiction writer who spins tales of fantasy, horror, romance, and mystery. Her short stories have been published in numerous magazines and anthologies, including *Hoosier Noir, Trick or Treat: Tales of All Hallows' Eve, Asinine Assassins, Between the Covers*, and the *The Big Fang*. When not writing, she cares for feral cats and other wildlife, reads, and strategizes imaginative ways for characters and trouble to collide

Liam Hogan is an award-winning short story writer, with stories in *Best of British Science Fiction*, and *Best of British Fantasy* (NewCon Press). He's been published by *Analog*, *Daily Science Fiction*, and *Flame Tree Press*, among others. He helps host Liars'

League London, volunteers at the creative writing charity Ministry of Stories, and lives and avoids work in London. More details at http://happyendingnotguaranteed.blogspot.co.uk

James Ryan has published the novel *Red Jenny and the Pirates of Buffalo*, as well as the popular history *The Pirates of New York*. He has also appeared in the publications *Pyramid Online*, *Dragon*, *The Urbanite*, *The Dream Zone*, *Rational Magic*, *REBEAT Magazine* where he had the column *Fantasia Obscura*, and *Rooftop Sessions*, the stories from which have been anthologized into the book *Alt Together Now*.

John Cady was born and raised in Southeastern Massachusetts. When he's not teaching English to incarcerated youth, he is either writing or making memories with his family. His works have been included in such anthologies as *After The Kool Aid Is Gon*e, *The ABC's of Terror Vol. 3*, and *Night Terrors Vol. 13*. His debut YA novella, *Attack of the 3-D Zombies*, was released in January 2022.

Michael McCormick writes stories in his Batman pajamas. Mike's work has appeared in *Arcanist, Daily SF, DreamForge, Frozen Wavelets, Grievous Angel, Metastellar, Talking Stick*, and elsewhere. Find out more at www.mikemccormick.org.

L. P. Melling currently writes from the East of England, UK, after academia and a legal careers took him around the country. His fiction has appeared in several places, including ASM, Hybrid Fiction, Shoreline of Infinity, and the Best of Anthology: The Future Looms. When not writing, he works for a legal charity in Cambridge. You can find out more about him at his website: www.lpmelling.wordpress.com

Tim Newton Anderson is a former daily newspaper journalist and PR executive who has recently started writing fiction. In the past year he has had 21 stories accepted for publication in outlets like

Emanations, Parsec, and Tales of the Shadowmen. Some of the stories were written as part of a self-challenge to write a story a week during lockdown, many based on suggestions of genre, lead character and location by the public via social media.

Ann Stolinshky's most recent publishing credit is a story accepted by Legion House Press for their anthology. Several short stories have been published in various anthologies. Three of those anthologies are going to the moon with Writers on the Moon. Ann is a member of the Writers Coffeehouse in Willow Grove, PA, and a critique group. She is also is a partner in Gemini Wordsmiths, a copyediting and content creation company. Gemini Wordsmiths formed a publishing imprint, Celestial Echo Press. Their first anthology, *The Twofer Compendium*, was published in December 2019. Their second, *The Trench Coat Chronicles*, was published in December 2020. In October 2021 they published George W. Young's debut novel, *TIME Blinked*. George's next novel, *DracuLAND*, is scheduled for a Hallowe'en 2022 release.

Ginger Strivelli has written for Marion Zimmer Bradley's Fantasy Magazine, Autism Parenting Magazine, Flash Fiction Magazine, Third Flatiron, Jokes Review, The New Accelerator, Cabinet of Heed Literary Journal, and several other publications. her most recent story was published in Frontier Tales' 2021 July issue.

Georgia Cook is an illustrator and writer from London. She is the winner of the LISP 2020 Flash Fiction Prize, and has been shortlisted for the Bridport Prize and Reflex Fiction Award, among others. She has also written for numerous podcasts, webcomics and anthologies. She can be found on twitter at @georgiacooked and on her website at https://www.georgiacookwriter.com/

DJ Tyrer is the person behind Atlantean Publishing and has been widely published in anthologies and magazines around the world, such as Chilling Horror Short Stories (Flame Tree), All The Petty

Myths (18th Wall), Steampunk Cthulhu (Chaosium), and EOM: Equal Opportunity Madness (Otter Libris), and issues of Hypnos, Occult Detective Magazine, parABnormal, and Weirdbook, and in addition, has a novella available in paperback and on the Kindle, The Yellow House (Dunhams Manor). DJ Tyrer's website is at https://djtyrer.blogspot.co.uk/DJ Tyrer's Facebook page is at https://www.facebook.com/DJTyrerwriter/

Claire Davon, a USA Today Bestselling author, has written on and off most of her life, starting with fan fiction when she was young. She writes across a wide range of genres. If a story calls to her, she writes it.

Donna J. W. Munro's pieces are published in Nothing's Sacred Magazine IV and V, Corvid Queen, Hazard Yet Forward (2012), Enter the *Apocalypse* (2017), B*eautiful Lies, Painful Truths II* (2018), *Terror Politico* (2019), *It Calls from the Forest* (2020), *Gray Sisters* Vol 1(2020), Borderlands Vol 7 (2020), P*seudopod 752* (2021), and others. Check out her first novel, *Revelation*: Poppet Cycle Book 1. Contact her at https://www.donnajwmunro.com or @DonnaJWMunro on Twitter.

Diane Arrelle, the pen name of Southern New Jersey writer Dina Leacock, has sold more than 350 short stories and has two short story collections: *Just A Drop In The Cup* and *Seasons On The Dark Side.* She resides with her sane husband and her insane cat on the edge of the Jersey Pine Barrens (home of the Jersey Devil).

Christopher Ryan has been an award-winning journalist, teacher, and writer. He has also been a podcaster, actor, producer, and director. But mostly he writes fast-paced stories with humor and heart. His most recent work includes articles and profiles for pulpfest.com, and short stories in the recently published *Now There Was a Story* anthology of crime fiction based on Johnny Cash music from Uncle B. Publications and *California Schemin*' the 2020 Bouchercon anthology. For more information, check out on social media @ chrisryanwrites.

Willow Croft is a freelance writer who currently lives out on the prairie but dreams of a home by a tumultuous ocean. She's had short stories published in Mad Scientist Journal, Speculative 66, Sirens Call eZine, Rock N' Roll Horror Zine, and in a number of anthologies. When not writing, she cares for some (very lucky) rescued street cats. Visit her at her blog, https://willowcroft.blog.

Michael H. Hanson created the ongoing *Sha'daa* shared-world anthology series currently consisting of *Sha'daa: Tales of the Apocalypse*, *Sha'daa: Last Call, Sha'daa: Pawns, Sha'daa: Facets, Sha'daa: Inked,* and *Sha'daa: Toys*, all published by Moondream Press (an imprint of Copper Dog Publishing). In 2017, Michael's short story *C.H.A.D.* appeared in the Eric S. Brown edited anthology *C.H.U.D. Lives!* (Crystal Lake Publishing), his short story R*ock and Road* appeared in the Roger Zelazny tribute anthology Shadows And Reflections, (Positronic Publishing) and his short story *Born of Dark Waters* appeared in the *The Beauty of Death* 2: *Death by Water* anthology (Independent Legions Press).Michael also has stories in Janet Morris's *Heroes in He*ll (HIH) anthology volumes (Perseid Press), *Lawyers in Hell, Rogues in Hell, Dreamers in Hell, Poets in Hell, Doctors In Hell, Pirates in Hel*l, and the recently published *Lovers in Hell.* Michael has had over 100 short stories published in the fields of horror, science fiction, and fantasy.

Acknowledgements

Thanks to:

All the authors who worked so hard to make TREES possible;

Rhyss DeCassilene for helping edit the first draft;

Tom for putting up with all the angst involved with getting TREES to print;

Stephen our webmaster;

Beverly Haaf who got TREES to print without me driving her completely and totally insane;

Lynell Kelly, Matt J. McGee, Christopher Ryan and Tim Newton Anderson for additional editing.

For Your Reading Pleasure
Jersey Pines Ink offers:

Seasons on the Dark Side, a Horror Short Story Collection by Diane Arrelle

Just A Drop In The Cup, a Collection of 42 Speculative and Mystery Short Stories by Diane Arrelle

WhoDunit, an Anthology of 42 Entertaining Mystery and Suspense Short Stories Edited by Dina Leacock

Crypt Gnats, an Anthology of the Horror Stories You've Been Itching To Read, Edited by Dina Leacock

The Chanting, a Novel of Supernatural Mystery and Romance by Beverly T. Haaf

Honeycomb Fire, a Novel of Adventure, Danger and Romance by Beverly T. Haaf

The JumpRope Chronicles, a Novel Series of Mystery and Romance in a Small Town by Ivy C. Leigh

Death Behind the Lilacs
Death Counts the Golden Coins
Death Spins an Indigo Web
Jump Into, an E-Book of short stories:
Coming Soon: ***Death Wears Red Roses***

https://www.jerseypinesink.com/